It took her a minute to adjust her eyes to the dim light, but she finally began making out shapes. Wheeled racks—some with empty hangers, some with clothes—stood behind a table piled with jeans. Stacked cartons mixed with other forms and silhouettes that weren't as easy to identify. Nancy took her penlight out of her blazer pocket and aimed it around the room. The thin but very bright light shot like a laser through the shadows.

She started slowly across the room, sweeping the shining light back and forth across the floor in front of her. Just ahead, two tall columns of stacked boxes defined a narrow path. As she stepped between the columns, she felt a wisp of air graze her cheek. Something else was in this room—something that was *breathing*.

Nancy turned her head slightly. One of the shadows seemed to move slightly. Or did it? Nancy's pulse pounded against the skin of her throat. She raised the penlight beam toward the shaking shadow.

Nancy Drew
Mystery Stories

Available from Simon & Schuster

NANCY DREW® 169

THE MISTLETOE MYSTERY

CAROLYN KEENE

Aladdin Paperbacks
New York   London   Toronto   Sydney   Singapore

First Aladdin Paperbacks edition November 2002

Copyright © 2002 by Simon & Schuster, Inc.

ALADDIN PAPERBACKS
An imprint of Simon & Schuster
Children's Publishing Division
1230 Avenue of the Americas
New York, NY 10020

Printed in the United States of America

10 9 8 7 6 5 4 3 2 1

NANCY DREW, NANCY DREW MYSTERY STORIES, and colophon
are registered trademarks of Simon & Schuster, Inc.

Library of Congress Control Number 2002101534

ISBN 0-7434-3765-9

Contents

THE MISTLETOE MYSTERY

1

Deck the Halls

"Albemarle's is kind of late with the whole holiday decorating thing, isn't it? All the other stores start right after Halloween." George Fayne's lanky, athletic stride set the pace as she and Nancy Drew walked across the parking lot toward Albemarle's department store.

"I know," Nancy said. "But the decorations are always so cool, it's worth the wait."

It was a day in late November. It didn't feel like autumn anymore, but it still wasn't really winter either. Nancy's blue down jacket felt good against the brisk wind. The bright sun reflected off her reddish blond hair. With her slim, fit body, she had no trouble keeping up with George.

"Well, with Bess working on the decorating crew,

they may never finish," George pointed out. "She can take forever with something like that."

Nancy opened the heavy brass-trimmed door, and they entered the store. Albemarle's was the oldest store in River Heights, and now the great-grandson of the founder was running the place. The first floor was two stories high and filled with display cases trimmed in dark wood. Huge, old-fashioned glass chandeliers cast a warm glow over the room.

A large balcony—the mezzanine—projected from two walls and hung over the first floor. An eyeglasses department, luggage displays, and a tea room were located on the mezzanine.

"Geez, this place is really jumping for a Wednesday," George said, watching dozens of shoppers darting from counter to counter. "Looks like everybody's got the holiday spirit."

Nancy looked around the huge room, assessing the people she saw—young men and women on lunch break from their jobs, mothers or fathers with small children, and college students between classes. She also saw a lot of people in their teens. It was the week of State High School Teachers Convention, and students got a few days' break from school.

Nancy and George walked up the wide stairway that led to the mezzanine.

"Yay, you made it!" Bess Marvin's cheery voice cut through the hum of the lunch crowd in the tea room.

She wore a green blazer, and her curly blond hair spilled over the collar. "Hurry," Bess urged her friends. "I can't wait till you meet Ali."

Nancy and George zigzagged over to Bess's table. "Nancy, where did you get that jacket?" Bess asked. "It matches your eyes. And mine! I definitely have to borrow it sometime."

"Albemarle's, of course," Nancy answered as she and George took their seats. The chairs were comfy with navy blue velvet upholstery and cream-painted wooden arms and legs.

Nancy smiled when she looked at Bess and George, her two best friends. Sometimes people were surprised to hear that Bess was George's cousin, because they were so different in every way. Both were Nancy's age—eighteen—but Bess was shorter and heavier than George. Her bubbly personality contrasted with George's no-nonsense manner.

"Ali, these are my dearest friends in the whole world," Bess said, introducing Nancy and George to Ali Marie. "I was at camp with Ali when I was ten years old," Bess explained, "and we haven't seen each other since. She was sixteen then, and one of the junior counselors. It was so great to run into her here at the store! She works in the junior's department—I think it's called WAVE."

Nancy knew that Albemarle's named some of their departments to give them a special feel, more like a small boutique. She had shopped at WAVE, which was a special department on the second floor catering to young adults who wanted to keep up with the latest trends.

"You'll have to check our department out while you're here," Ali said. "We've got some really cool new holiday stuff." She was very pretty, with wavy auburn hair and large gray-blue eyes. She was wearing fitted black pants and a crisp white shirt.

"Ali is on the executive track here," Bess reported. She paused while the four gave their lunch orders to the waitress. "She's going to be a buyer," Bess concluded when the waitress left.

"Well, that's one goal," Ali said. "But first I have to get through the holiday season—and it can be really wild. This time of year it's all about sales, promotions, and crazy shoppers. We slashed the prices for a special sale once, and two girls fought so hard over a skirt that they ripped it right in two."

"Sort of gives new meaning to the word 'slash' right?" George observed with a clever smile.

"Exactly," Ali said, grinning. "I really shouldn't be laughing, because it just contributes to the overall shrinkage, but it *was* funny."

"Shrinkage," Bess repeated. "What does that mean?"

The waitress served them their hamburgers, fries, and sodas while Ali explained. "'Shrinkage' is the store security word for all merchandise that is lost for some reason or another—shoplifting, damage, whatever."

"Shoplifting can be more of a problem during the holiday season," Nancy pointed out. "Most department stores base their whole revenue predictions and budgets on their holiday sales. Lots of special promotions bring in more customers. And the more shoppers there are, the easier it is for thieves to hide what they're doing."

"But the store knows that, right?" Bess asked. "Don't they add more detectives and security people during the holiday season?"

"That helps a lot," Ali said, nodding. "Albemarle's added a few extra people." She leaned in toward the others. "But we've had some problems already—in the electronics department. I just heard this morning that some very expensive stuff is missing from their stockroom: high-end minicomputers, handhelds, business machines, even surveillance equipment."

"That sounds like more than light shoplifting," Nancy said. "Or maybe it's shoplifting with an insider as a connection."

"You mean an Albemarle's employee?" George asked, taking a bite of her sandwich.

"Mmm-hmm," Nancy answered. "Or someone actually breaking in at night."

"Have you ever seen someone steal something, Ali?" Bess asked.

"I've certainly seen some pretty suspicious people,"

Ali said, "especially since we started our party clothes promotion over the last few days. But I've never seen someone actually stick something in a purse or under a coat or whatever. There has been one woman sort of hanging around lately. I think she acts weird, and she's never bought anything while I'm on the floor. I told my manager about it, but she thinks I'm imagining things."

"Well, Nancy's the best detective in River Heights," Bess exclaimed. "If Albemarle's had any sense, they'd have her working undercover to watch over their stuff."

Bess and George told Ali about a few of Nancy's past cases while they ate their lunch. Then the conversation switched to clothes and some of the new trends.

"We've got some new Ellen-Louise party dresses in that are so cool," Ali mentioned.

"They're gorgeous," Bess agreed. "But there's no way I can afford them. I did get a scarf, though."

"Which reminds me," Ali said, checking her watch. "It's two o'clock already. I'd better get back to work."

"Me too," Bess declared, jumping up. "At least I don't have far to go." She pointed to the opposite end of the mezzanine, where Nancy could see people hanging garlands of dark green tied with large burgundy bows. "Are you two going to hang out for a while?" she asked Nancy and George.

"Actually, I'm headed to WAVE to look for a sweater," Nancy answered.

"And I'm checking out some golf clubs," George said.

"In the winter?" Bess asked.

"Hey, I know what I'm doing," George said. "Golf stuff will be on super-sale. See you later!"

Nancy and Bess walked to the stairway. "Stop by before you leave," Bess urged Nancy before she walked over to the decorating crew.

Nancy went back down the mezzanine stairway to the first floor, then took the escalator up to WAVE on the second floor. The entrance to the department was an arch created by a large blue crashing wave. Ali was busy with another customer, so Nancy looked at sweaters. As she held up a soft red one in front of a mirror, Ali joined her.

"There," Ali whispered as she met Nancy's gaze in the mirror. "See that woman over your left shoulder?"

Nancy looked in the mirror at the reflection of a woman in a black coat with wooden buttons.

"She's the one I was talking about at lunch," Ali said, her voice still low. "The woman who hangs around but never buys anything. I don't think she's a shopper."

Nancy watched the woman leafing through some merino wool blazers hanging from a rod tucked into a wall alcove. She had straight, almost-black hair in an earlobe-length bob. Occasionally the woman would glance around at the other shoppers as if she felt someone watching her.

Ali was called away, but Nancy stayed at her vantage point in front of the mirror. She turned and posed, holding the sweater in front of her, but watching the woman in the reflection. Occasionally Nancy pretended to study the sweater's stitching or label. Once when she looked up, the woman was staring at her in the mirror. Nancy looked away and then back, and the woman was gone.

Nancy looked around and saw the woman's head bobbing away through the crowd. Nancy couldn't resist checking out the woman that Ali thought was suspicious. "Hold this for me," she told Ali, handing her the sweater. "I'll be right back."

Nancy followed the woman out of WAVE and across the second floor to the escalator. They both rode down to the first floor, Nancy about ten steps behind the woman. The woman took a seat in the shoe department and began talking to one of the saleswomen.

Nancy ducked into the hosiery department nearby, where she could keep an eye on the woman. While Nancy looked at socks and stockings, she watched as the woman began trying on shoes. Minutes passed. The woman seemed to be preparing for a long stay in the shoe department. Nancy watched as she took off the black coat with the wooden buttons and draped it over a nearby chair. The saleswoman emerged from the stockroom nearly hidden by a double stack of shoeboxes.

Looks like she might be a shopper after all, Nancy thought. She watched a few minutes longer, then decided to head back upstairs.

When Nancy returned to WAVE, she spotted Ali across the room. She was pointing toward the corner as she spoke to a woman seated behind a sleek chrome sales desk. As Nancy approached them, the sound of Ali's voice pierced through the funky music shaking from the speakers on the wall.

"They're gone, Diedra!" Ali said. "All of them. Someone has stolen all the Ellen-Louise gowns!"

2

The Weather Outside Is Frightful

"What happened?" Nancy asked, rushing to Ali's side.

"Oh, Nancy, it's awful." Ali's words stumbled out in short bursts. "The Ellen-Louise dresses. Our best designer line. The most expensive. The most *gorgeous*. Someone stole them!"

"Ali!" the woman behind the desk stood up, interrupting Ali's staccato report. Ali gave Nancy one last look of distress. Then she took a deep breath, shook her head, and continued in a calmer voice. "Nancy, this is my manager, Diedra Haize. Diedra, my friend Nancy Drew."

"I'm happy to meet you," Diedra said with a smile. She looked like she was in her early thirties, and was dressed smartly in a long skirt and cardigan. "Now, if you'll excuse us." She took Nancy's elbow firmly and walked her several yards away from the desk. Then she returned to Ali, steering her toward the corner as Diedra dialed a number on her cell phone with one hand.

Nancy watched as Ali and Diedra talked in low voices. Diedra seemed to balance two conversations—one with Ali, and one on her phone.

Diedra closed her phone, and she and Ali hurried through an arched opening in the corner. Within minutes, a man strode quickly into WAVE. He was tall, with wavy silver hair. The man was greeted by Ali and Diedra when they re-entered the room. The three huddled briefly before Ali came over to get Nancy.

"Nancy, he wants to talk to you," she said breathlessly. "I told him about the strange woman and how you were sort of watching her."

"Hello, Nancy," the man said warmly, holding out his hand. "I'm Jack Lee, Albemarle's chief of security. We haven't met, but I've heard about you. You've got quite a reputation in security circles. Nearly every detective I know in River Heights seems to have gotten your help at least once."

"I hear this is a busy time of year for you, Mr. Lee," Nancy said, shaking his hand.

"Unfortunately that's true," he replied. "And please, call me Jack." His glance darted to Ali and then back to Nancy. "Ali tells me you've been on a stakeout this afternoon."

"I wouldn't call it that exactly," Nancy said. "Ali just mentioned a woman she believed had been acting suspiciously."

"Was she that dark-haired woman you mentioned to me?" Diedra asked Ali. She sounded impatient.

"Well, yes, but—" Ali began.

"Just tell me what you saw that made you suspicious," Jack urged Ali.

Ali repeated what she had told Nancy. Then Nancy added her own observations, which she realized didn't add up to much. Diedra joined in, saying she had never seen the woman in question doing anything wrong. But she admitted the woman did seem to hang around a lot and never bought anything.

"I see," Jack said with a sigh. Nancy could tell by his tone of voice that he wasn't impressed with Ali's theory. He turned to Nancy and gave her a broad smile. "I sure appreciate your efforts here, Nancy, but it looks like you might have been wasting your time."

"But how do you know?" Ali asked. "We all know what's happened in the electronics department. And now *our* best merchandise has been stolen. How do you know this woman wasn't involved?"

"You are right to report any behavior you think might be suspicious," Jack answered. "But, with all due respect to Nancy's great reputation, we can handle Albemarle's security without the help of freelancers."

"You told me the majority of shrinkage these days is caused by employee activity, and you thought what's been happening here lately is an inside job," Diedra said to Jack. "Do you still think so?"

"You think an employee is behind this?" Ali said.

"Okay, let's just wind this up for now," Jack said. "Nancy and Ali, thanks again for your help. And we'd appreciate your keeping this quiet. We'll take it from here. Diedra, show me where the stolen dresses were hanging."

Diedra bustled into action, leading Jack to the arched opening in the corner.

"Nancy, I'm sorry," Ali said. "I didn't mean to embarrass you. I just thought . . . well, if that woman *was* a shoplifter, wouldn't it be cool if you and I could capture her?"

"It's okay, Ali," Nancy said. "But before I leave, tell me exactly what you found when you discovered the dresses had been stolen."

"I went into the storeroom to wheel out the rack," Ali said. "The dresses arrived this morning, and I sent them out to be freshly pressed. Oh, Nancy, they're so beautiful. Ellen-Louise creates the greatest designs. I spent all morning planning how to display her dresses."

"And they weren't there when you got to the storeroom?" Nancy prompted.

"Diedra told me they'd been delivered from the

presser," Ali said, her hands shaking. "I walked into the storeroom, and they were gone. The cables were cut and just hanging there."

"Security cables," Nancy repeated, walking over to a designer display in a set created to look like a young woman's clothes closet. All of the garments were attached by cables to the display. "Like these?" she asked, running her fingers over a thin silver-colored cord.

"Yes. They're electronic cables, and they sound an alarm if they're cut. The most expensive clothes also have these tags," Ali added, pulling out a tag that was hidden deep in the sleeve of a crisp white shirt. "These sound alarms too, if they're messed with. But we never heard a sound."

"Hmmmm," Nancy murmured. "You and the other employees know how to disarm the alarms. You can remove the tags and disconnect the cables without activating the security system, right?"

"Sure," Ali said. "Oh, I see what you mean. If we didn't hear the alarm, it must have been fixed to not go off. So it would have to be an employee who took the dresses."

"It wouldn't *have* to be," Nancy said, shaking her head. "Thieves often learn how to get around security systems. But employees can definitely disarm them. Anyway, it would be impossible for a shoplifter to hide a whole rack of party dresses and walk out."

14

"Maybe she has an accomplice!" Ali said.

"Ali, we've got to be careful about accusing people," Nancy warned. "We have no evidence that this woman has done anything wrong. We should take Jack's advice and just back off. Let the security staff take care of it."

Nancy paid for the sweater Ali had held for her, and left WAVE. She rode down the escalator to the first floor, then walked up the steps to the mezzanine. Bess and another young woman were hanging evergreen boughs on the walls.

"Hey, Nancy," Bess called. "Is this beautiful or what?" She pointed to some of the decorations. "I wish I could take a break, but I can't. One of our crew members went home with the flu, and who knows when he'll get back. We're all doing double duty till then."

"That's okay," Nancy said. "Just keep working." The other young woman left to get more boughs from a large box at the end of the mezzanine. While she was gone, Nancy quickly told Bess about the stolen dresses from WAVE.

"Wow! Poor Ali," Bess said.

"Don't tell anyone else about this yet," Nancy warned as the other crew member returned, armed with more greenery. She was tall and very slim, with short light-brown hair.

Bess introduced Nancy. "And this is Cassandra

15

Anderson—we call her Cass," she continued. "She's a full-time employee of the decorating company called Special Effects. We're going to be—"

"Girls. Girls!" A stocky man with a pink face bustled over. "What are you doing? Please get to work—you know we're in trouble here. We've got to meet the deadline, and we're already short one decorator. *Please.*"

"This is Wayne Weber," Bess said to Nancy. "Wayne's the owner of Special Effects, and the genius behind all these beautiful decorations."

"Thank you, thank you," Wayne said. "Now can I please talk you into getting back to work?" He turned to Nancy. "No offense, but I need these girls to buckle down and start hanging."

While he talked, Nancy had an idea. "Excuse me," she said. "Maybe I could help. I've had decorating experience." She gave Bess a quick look. "And I'm free the next few days. I could start immediately, and fill in for your sick crew member."

Wayne looked at Nancy, and seemed to be sizing her up. "Well . . . ," he began.

Nancy shot Bess another look, and Bess stepped up. "She'll be a big help, Wayne," she said. "Nancy's got a real flair for decorating."

Wayne looked at Bess, then back at Nancy. He quoted her an hourly rate, Nancy nodded, and he nodded back. "Fine," he said, looking at his watch.

"You start now. Finish with the boughs. Bess can get you a locker and an employee blazer." With a quick smile, he turned and walked briskly toward the stairs.

Nancy, Bess, and Cass worked for hours, draping and hanging the boughs around the walls of the mezzanine. By the time they finished, it was nearly seven o'clock.

Nancy was disappointed to hear that the Special Effects crew was quitting early that night. She had hoped to spend some time in the store after hours. She, Bess, and Cass gathered the empty boxes that had held the greenery and the tools they'd used for hanging. Then they carried them down to a large storeroom on the lowest level—the basement—of the store.

"This is temporary headquarters for Special Effects," Bess explained. "Find a blazer from that rack," she said.

Nancy found a green blazer in her size and tried it on. Like the others, it had "Special Effects" sewn on one pocket.

"That looks perfect," Bess said. "We always wear the jacket while we're working, and we're supposed to wear a white shirt and black pants with it."

She followed Bess to the back wall, which was lined with a double row of lockers. Nancy took the key from one locker and strung it onto her key ring.

17

Cass left to join the other crew members, and Bess and Nancy were alone in the huge storeroom. The room was crammed with boxes printed with the Special Effects logo. A peek inside revealed coiled garlands of artificial greenery, piles of wire ready to be molded into shapes, gold fruit sparkling with glitter, vivid red flowers, and bells covered with tiny mirrors.

Other boxes were unmarked, except for the word "Holidays" handwritten in black marker. "Those are the boxes of old Albemarle's decorations," Bess said of the hand-labeled boxes. "Most of the things are really shabby—I don't know why they're hanging on to them. These, however, are so cool. . . ."

Bess pulled back several drapes of fabric to reveal a dozen nearly life-size figures. A family of four dressed in velvet coats and furry hats, a Great Dane on a red leash, a black cat with white feet, a pony pulling a sleigh, three strolling singers holding books of music, a snowman, and a policeman in an old-fashioned uniform directed their glass-eyed gaze at Nancy.

"These are fantastic," Nancy said. "I see hinges on their bodies. They must be mechanical."

"They are," Bess said. "Watch." She plugged a large electrical console into a wall socket, then flipped a lever on the console. A faint whirring noise filtered through the air. Then the figures came to life. The heads of the father and children turned and bowed. The mother's hand came up to her mouth, and her eyes blinked rapidly.

"This is great," Nancy said. As she watched, one of the father's arms pulled on the red leash. The Great Dane's tail wagged as he strained toward the cat. The cat stood on its back legs and batted its front paws in the air.

"I know," Bess said, with a grin. "I'm not supposed to mess with these, but Cass showed me how to turn them on." The mechanical pony pulled the sleigh forward and backward while it shook its head from side to side. The policeman reached for the pony's bridle over and over, but never quite grasped it. Even the snowman's hat popped up and down on his head.

"I've never seen anything like these," Nancy said. "But they look really old. Did Albemarle's use these figures a long time ago?" Nancy asked. "Or did Wayne bring them from Special Effects?"

"They belong to Albemarle's," Bess said, turning off the figures and unplugging the console. "Wayne's thinking about using them, but we don't know how yet."

Nancy helped Bess cover the figures, and then they walked to the store parking lot. It was about eight o'clock. Tall lights made irregular patterns around the lot. Without the sun, it seemed like winter after all. The wind was biting cold against Nancy's cheeks, and she noticed that a thin layer of ice covered the ground. "I'll pick you up in the morning," Nancy said, her breath puffing out in whitish spurts.

"We need to be here at nine o'clock," Bess answered. "The store doesn't open till ten, so we go in the employees' entrance at the back."

"Okay, see you about eight-thirty." They walked in opposite directions to their cars. As Nancy weaved through the light and shadows, she felt someone nearby. "Bess?" she called out. "Is that you?" She stopped walking and listened carefully. The cold, clear night was very still.

Nancy walked quicker now, heading toward her blue Mustang. Slowly she became aware of an odd noise—it sounded like someone taking quick gulps of the icy air. She darted between two cars and ducked down.

It was now very quiet. Nancy raised her head so she could look around. No one was in sight. Crouching down so she could shield herself behind the cars, Nancy crept toward her Mustang. When she got to her car, she pushed her car key firmly into the lock. She stabbed at the lock multiple times—but the key would not go in.

3

Catching the WAVE

Maybe the lock's frozen, Nancy thought. She clicked on the small light on her key ring and aimed it toward the car door. Something metal inside the lock glinted out at her.

Nancy looked around. Uneasy—and eager to get away—she stepped quickly around to the passenger side. Her key glided smoothly into the door lock. She slid inside, moved over to the steering wheel, and drove out of Albemarle's parking lot.

She noticed no one following her home, but she still breathed easier when she was safe in her own garage. She rechecked the car lock on the driver's side. Whatever was jammed in there had not dislodged. She found small needlenose pliers in the toolbox and carefully pulled out the metal object.

She recognized it immediately as one of the tools she often used when she was on a case.

"The end of a lock pick," she murmured to herself. Her breath hung in frosty clouds in the unheated garage. "Someone broke off a lock pick in my car door. Who would break into my car? *Why?*"

When she finally got inside, she was greeted by Hannah Gruen's warm voice. "There you are," Hannah said. "Have you eaten? I'll fix up some dinner for you. Your father called. The consulting he's doing on that case in Chicago is taking longer than he thought. He won't be home until Sunday evening."

Nancy's father, Carson Drew, had hired Hannah to be the Drews' housekeeper when Nancy's mother died fifteen years ago. Carson was a very busy attorney and knew that Hannah would not only help keep the house running and cook the meals, but she would also be a comforting presence for Nancy.

"I'm definitely hungry," Nancy said. "I seem to have completely forgotten about dinner."

Hannah had a plate of fried chicken and homemade biscuits on the kitchen table by the time Nancy hung up her coat and unpacked her backpack. The two chatted about Nancy's day while they shared the warm, buttered biscuits.

"Working for the decorating crew will enable me to get behind the scenes at the store," Nancy told

Hannah. "Sometimes the crew stays after hours to decorate."

"So you *are* interested in the thefts going on at the store," Hannah said, "in spite of telling Ali that you should probably back off?"

"Mmm-hmm," Nancy said, taking a gulp of milk.

Nancy decided to keep the lock-picking attempt a secret for now. She didn't want to worry Hannah, and she didn't really have much to tell her about it anyway.

"Well, I've watched you solve many cases over the years," Hannah said. "And I'll give the same advice I always do: Be careful!"

When she finished her supper, Nancy called George and told her about the theft of the Ellen-Louise dresses, her signing on to work with Special Effects, and the attempt to break into her car. George offered to help in any way she could.

Thursday morning, Nancy and Bess were the first decorators to arrive at the Albemarle's parking lot. While Bess waited for the others, Nancy retraced the steps she took the previous evening, scanning the ground carefully.

"Did you find anything?" Bess asked when Nancy rejoined her friend outside Albemarle's door.

"Nothing," Nancy whispered. "Not a clue about who tried to break into my car yesterday."

Wayne drove up in a medium-size truck with "Special Effects" written on the side in elegant black script. He ushered his crew into the store and down to their temporary headquarters in the basement stockroom. Checking his clipboard, Wayne assigned tasks to the members of his crew. "And when you're all finished with those projects," Wayne told everyone, "check with me on the mezzanine."

Nancy and Bess were asked to fill huge vases with red and gold flowers on the first floor. The vases were made to look like ancient Roman urns. They were really created from a very lightweight material so they could be moved easily.

The vases sat on pedestals, about six feet off the floor. Nancy and Bess climbed stepladders so they could reach the top of the urns. Then they followed Wayne's detailed diagram for placing the red and gold flowers and branches in the vases.

While they worked, Nancy and Bess talked quietly about Nancy's scare in the parking lot and the thefts from WAVE.

"I'm really worried about Ali," Bess told Nancy. "She's so upset about the missing dresses. She feels really guilty because it happened while she was there. She can't believe it happened right under her nose."

Bess handed Nancy a large red velvet flower and two gold branches. "Cass has a friend working in the young men's department, and he says a lot of sales-

24

people think the thefts are an inside job."

"That's what Jack Lee thinks," Nancy said, pushing the flower and branches down into the large vase. "And it makes sense to me. Do Cass or her friends have any suspects?"

"They think it might be Diedra, Ali's boss."

"Really?" Nancy said, remembering her conversation with Diedra and how the woman seemed eager to hustle Nancy out of the area. "Does anyone have a motive for her, a reason why she'd do it?"

"Cass didn't say," Bess answered.

"Then there may be nothing to the gossip," Nancy said. "But I'd like to talk to Cass's friend anyway. I'll get his name and—"

"Nancy! Bess!" Ali interrupted Nancy. From their high vantage point, they saw Ali running around the cosmetics counters toward them.

"What's wrong?" Nancy asked as she and Bess scurried down the ladders.

Ali's face scrunched into lines and ridges as she looked at them.

"I've been fired!"

"No!" Bess said. "They wouldn't fire you. You're a star employee."

"Well, they did it anyway," Ali said, her voice harsh with anger. "I can't believe it!"

"What reason did they give?" Nancy asked. She saw tears welling in Ali's eyes.

"They didn't even call it firing," Ali said. "But it was. Diedra said that Albemarle's needs to cut back, so they had to let me go."

"That doesn't make sense," Nancy said. "The store's been running ads for weeks, trying to hire more salespeople to handle the holiday crowds."

"Exactly," Ali said.

"Ali, do you think it has anything to do with the missing merchandise?" Nancy asked gently.

Tears started to creep down Ali's cheeks. "Diedra didn't say that exactly," Ali said. "But she acted so weird. I think they blame me. They think *I* stole the gowns!"

"Surely they don't think that," Bess said, putting her arm around Ali's shoulder. She turned to Nancy. "We have to help her. I know Ali—she would never do something like this."

"If they had any real evidence against you, they probably would have arrested you," Nancy said.

"But even if they think I did it but can't prove it, I'm ruined." Ali pointed out. "I'm set up for a career in retail. I can't afford to have even a suspicion of this kind of crime on my record."

"I'll see what I can find out," Nancy assured Ali. "We work until closing tonight. Let's meet after that, and we can talk more about it. How about Scarletti's, for pizza? I'll call George and ask her to come too."

After Ali left, Nancy and Bess got back to work.

Soon it was time for their one o'clock lunch break. After taking the boxes of decorations back to a storeroom on the first floor, Bess went to the mezzanine for lunch with some of the other decorating crew members. Nancy decided to grab an energy bar from her backpack and use the time to talk to a few of Albemarle's employees.

Cass had given Nancy the name of a friend in the young men's department. Nancy headed there first. She located Cass's friend quickly by his name tag.

"Hi, Ron," she said. "I'm Nancy. I'm part of the crew that's setting up the holiday decorations for the store. Cass Anderson told me to look you up. I'm looking for a present for a friend."

"Sure," he said. "You got anything in mind?"

"Maybe a shirt," Nancy said, looking through a display.

"What size do you need?"

"Medium," Nancy answered, holding up a green shirt with a hood and zip front. "Pretty weird about all the thefts around the store lately, isn't it? Has anything happened in your department?"

"Not so far," he answered. "Did you hear about the damage someone did to WAVE?"

"I did," Nancy said. "Cass thinks Diedra Haize might have something to do with it."

Ron moved closer to Nancy and lowered his voice. "I think so too," he said. He looked around to make sure no one was eavesdropping on them. "Diedra's been looking to be store manager. She's worked hard for Albemarle's, and everyone thought she'd get it when the job opened up last summer."

"What happened?" Nancy asked.

"They gave the job to someone in the Albemarle family," Ron answered. "He's okay, I guess, but he's never even worked here. Diedra really knows the setup, and she would have been great."

"But you think she robbed the store for some kind of revenge?" Nancy reminded him. "Doesn't sound like she'd be a good store manager."

"Yeah, I guess you're right," Ron said. "All I'm saying is, she had a motive. And you have to admit—since she's the head of WAVE, she sure had the prime opportunity to take a few things."

Before she reported back to work, Nancy stopped by WAVE. She was glad to see Diedra wasn't around, so she could talk to some of the others in the department. She skillfully questioned several of Ali's coworkers before Diedra returned.

When Nancy returned to the main floor, Bess was waiting for her. They got back to work filling vases with beautiful arrangements. When they finally finished, they reported to Wayne on the mezzanine. It was six o'clock.

"Why don't you two take a dinner break," he suggested. "And then come back here. I'll need your help with the holly tree decorations."

Nancy and Bess walked down the mezzanine steps. "I want to look around WAVE," Nancy said. "Let's save dinner for Scarletti's later, okay?"

"Sure," Bess said.

Nancy led Bess across the room through the maze of display counters to the Up escalator.

"I want to check out the WAVE stockroom," Nancy said in a hushed voice. "But I don't want Diedra to see us. Stand guard from a distance, okay? If Diedra starts for the stockroom entrance, divert her attention. Ask her if Ali's left yet—pretend you don't know what's happened."

"What are you looking for?" Bess asked.

"I don't know," Nancy said. "Jack, and maybe even the police, have probably raked it for clues—but I want to take a look anyway. The Ellen-Louise dresses were taken in broad daylight, while the store was open. Ali said the gowns were there one minute, and gone the next. If that's true, the theft had to be done in a hurry. When you're in a hurry, you make mistakes—and some of those mistakes can be clues."

"Okay, let's go," Bess said. Nancy was proud of her friend's eagerness.

They climbed the steps to the second floor, and Nancy quietly opened the door. The department immediately in front of them was infants & toddlers. Nancy led Bess through the department, dodging the glances of the sales clerk. Using racks of clothing as shields, they worked their way around the room to WAVE.

Diedra was busy behind a counter, sorting cash and checks. Bess stepped behind the large arching blue wave at the entrance to the department, where she could safely watch both Diedra and the stockroom entrance.

Nancy waited patiently for an opportunity to dart into the stockroom. Finally it arrived with the chirpy beep of a cell phone ringing. Diedra reached into her pocket and pulled out her phone. Within seconds she was deep into a quiet conversation, her back turned toward the room and the stockroom door on the side wall.

Nancy darted around behind the WAVE display tables and sale racks, and stepped into the stockroom.

The room was dimly lit from a few small lights. It was like being in a room illuminated by night-lights plugged into the sockets. There was a light switch at the entrance, but Nancy knew she didn't dare turn it on. She stepped back against a dark wall and looked around.

It took her a minute to adjust her eyes to the dim light, but she finally began making out shapes.

Wheeled racks—some with empty hangers, some with clothes—stood behind a table piled with jeans. Stacked cartons mixed with other forms and silhouettes that weren't as easy to identify. Nancy took her penlight out of her blazer pocket and aimed it around the room. The thin but very bright light shot like a laser through the shadows.

She started slowly across the room, sweeping the shining light back and forth across the floor in front of her. Just ahead, two tall columns of stacked boxes defined a narrow path. As she stepped between the columns, she felt a wisp of air graze her cheek. Something else was in this room—something that was *breathing*.

Nancy turned her head slightly. One of the shadows seemed to move slightly. Or did it? Nancy's pulse pounded against the skin of her throat. She raised the penlight beam toward the shaking shadow.

4

Shreds of Evidence

As Nancy brought her penlight beam up, the shadowy form jerked into action. It rushed directly at her, smashing her into a rack of blouses and shorts.

Nancy's penlight flew out of her hand and skidded across the floor. Her arms flailed in front of her body—partly to try to keep her balance, and partly to defend herself. The shadow pushed harder, and Nancy's left leg buckled from the impact. As she fell backward, she grabbed on to what seemed to be her attacker's shirt.

Nancy tumbled backward. She felt a shock of pain as her shoulder hit the wall. She sank to the floor, her fall cushioned by a jumble of clothes. As Nancy landed, she felt the material in her fist rip away from the shadow. Stunned from the blow, Nancy watched the form race to the stockroom entrance, then creep out and disappear.

Nearly out of breath, Nancy scrambled to her feet and stumbled to the door. She looked out into the WAVE showroom. Bess was talking to Diedra, whose back was to Nancy. But there was no sign of anyone running away.

Neither Bess nor Diedra saw her, so she ducked back into the stockroom shadows. She found her penlight and turned it on. Not until then did she unclench her fist. Inside was a scrap of navy blue cloth. The stitching looked as if it might have been a pocket before Nancy tore it away.

Cradled in the material was what looked like a plastic triangle. Nancy pulled it closer to the light beam. It looked like the corner of a piece of paper laminated between two plastic sheets. Printed on the paper was the letter *e*. Below the letter were the numbers 701.

Nancy spent a few minutes exploring the rest of the stockroom, but found nothing unusual. When she returned to the doorway, she could hear that Diedra and Bess now seemed to be arguing. Diedra was still facing the other way. Bess saw Nancy, but didn't give her away.

Nancy darted between the displays until she was back at the entrance to WAVE. Pretending she was just arriving, she strode under the arched wave and across the floor to where Bess and Diedra stood.

"I know . . . I know you're really busy right now," Bess explained with a sweet smile. "I just wanted to talk with Ali. When will she be back?"

Diedra ignored her question and turned toward Nancy. "Can I help you with something?" Her voice seemed to indicate an increased level of frustration and impatience.

"Actually, I was looking for Bess," Nancy said. "And Ali," she added. "Has she left already?"

"You two are together?" Diedra said, looking from Nancy to Bess. Then she answered Nancy's question abruptly. "Yes, Ali has left." She began walking toward the entrance, as if to encourage Nancy and Bess to do the same.

"Oh, well, maybe we'll see her tomorrow," Nancy said, not moving from her place.

Diedra sighed. "That's not likely," she said. "Ali is no longer working here. Now if you'll both please leave—I really need to close up."

Nancy began walking slowly along with Diedra. Bess followed behind. "Did Ali quit?" Nancy asked. "That would really surprise me—she loves working here."

"You'll hear it soon enough, I guess," Diedra said. "Ali has been let go. We needed to cut back, unfortunately."

"I can't believe that," Nancy said, looking directly

into Diedra's eyes. "We all know that stores hire during the holidays—they don't fire people, especially star employees like Ali. Unless, of course, there's a problem. Like missing dresses, for instance. Come on, Diedra, you know that I know all about the theft. You can tell us the truth. Was Ali fired because of that?"

Diedre paused before speaking. "That probably had a lot to do with it, yes," she said, avoiding Nancy's gaze.

"But you surely don't think she had something to do with it," Bess said. "You *know* her. She'd never do anything like that."

"Look, it's out of my hands," Diedra said. "The whole thing is still under investigation. Maybe, if some more evidence turns up, things might change. But for now, Ali needs to be let go."

"An innocent person suffers," Bess said.

"If you had *any* evidence, Ali would be in jail. What makes you think she was involved?" Nancy asked.

"You'll have to ask Jack. This was his call. But Ali *was* here when they were stolen," Diedra answered. "And she had a motive."

"You were here when the dresses were stolen too," Nancy pointed out. She decided to take a chance with the information Ron had given her, and test Diedra's reaction. "And *you* also have a motive."

"That's it," Diedra said, clearly ruffled. "Leave. Now!"

The girls had by now reached the entrance to WAVE. Diedra returned to the counter.

Nancy and Bess walked to the escalator. As they rode down to the first floor, Nancy told Bess about her assault in the WAVE stockroom.

"We never heard a thing," Bess exclaimed. "Not a sound. And I didn't see anyone sneak out, either."

"I landed in a pile of clothes," Nancy reminded her. "It was like falling on a mattress, so there wasn't any crash. You and Diedra were talking by then, too, so I'm not surprised that you didn't hear our scuffle. I wish you'd seen my assailant leaving the scene, though. That would have been a big help."

"I probably would have if I'd still been at my prime observation post—behind the wave," Bess said. "But Diedra spotted me and began asking a lot of questions. I had to keep her talking so you could finish scoping out the stockroom."

"You did a great job," Nancy said. She and Bess walked to the mezzanine stairway and up the steps. "Especially by keeping her focused on you, instead of on the stockroom.

"What did Diedra mean when she said Ali had a motive?" Bess wondered. Nancy could see Wayne and the other crew members on the mezzanine ahead.

"I might have an idea about that," Nancy said. "I spent my lunch hour questioning Cass's friend in the young men's department, and some other WAVE employees. Later I'll tell you what I found out."

Nancy and Bess were asked to transport the decorations for what Wayne considered his masterpiece for the store: a giant holly tree, which was located next to the top of the mezzanine stairway. Hundreds of silver glass balls had to be securely fixed to the branches, and thousands of tiny white lights needed to be woven in and out of the leaves. The silver and white handmade imported glass ornaments that would also decorate the tree were Wayne's original designs.

Hundreds of boxes needed to be moved from the van to a locked supply closet on the mezzanine. There the decorations would be secure while the decorating proceeded. Wayne unlocked the big closet, which was about ten feet long and six feet wide. It was lined with shelves, which were empty except for a few boxes of menus from the tearoom.

Everyone helped move the boxes. All of them contained fragile items, so Wayne insisted they be brought in one at a time by hand, and not carted on a dolly. Nancy and Bess brought in the last four boxes. By the time they were finished it was eight o'clock, and Wayne called the workday over.

"I didn't think we'd ever finish," Bess said as she

and Nancy hurried from the mezzanine. "We're the last ones out of here. All that walking, and no dinner yet. I'm *so* hungry."

"Me too," Nancy said. "George and Ali are probably already at Scarletti's. Let's get out of here." They were the last to get their coats and gear.

"Are you going to call Jack Lee and tell him about the person who knocked you down?" Bess asked, as they walked to the Special Effects temporary headquarters.

"Yes, but there's no rush," Nancy said. "Whoever it was is long gone by now. I'll tell Mr. Lee in the morning."

No one was in the dark storeroom when they arrived. Nancy flicked the light switch, and the room was quickly filled with harsh fluorescent yellow light. Nancy and Bess went to their lockers to deposit their blazers and get their coats and bags.

"Hey, look at this," Bess said. A note was stuck in a slot in Bess's locker door. "It's from Ali," she reported. "'Tell Nancy I really appreciate you two helping me out,'" she read aloud. "There's a thank-you waiting for you both at the Millennium makeup counter."

"That's cool," Nancy said. "I like their stuff."

"Me too," Bess said, opening her locker. "I wear their lipstick all the time. . . . What's this?" Her cheery tone had changed dramatically. "Nancy . . . come here . . . my scarf," Bess said, reaching into the locker. She spoke very slowly, and she sounded very scared.

Nancy hurried to Bess's side. "Looks like you got another message," she said as they looked into the locker. Nancy felt an odd sensation from behind, as if they were being watched. She turned quickly, but saw no one.

"What is it?" Bess whispered. "Did you hear something?"

"I guess not," Nancy said, her voice low. She turned slowly back to Bess's locker. A beautiful soft pink scarf embossed with burgundy velvet leaves hung from Bess's hand in a tangle. Part of it had been torn into long, tattered shreds. Paperclipped to the scarf was a note with just two words: BACK OFF.

5

Undercover Decorator

"Oh, Nancy," Bess said, still whispering. "My new scarf! I just bought it for the holidays."

Nancy carefully placed the scarf and the anonymous note in an Albemarle's paper bag that she found stuffed in a corner of the closet. "We'll turn these over to Jack in the morning," she said. "Let's get out of here."

As she spoke she heard a scuffling noise and then a rapid clicking sound, like the tapping of nails on a table.

Bess's fingers dug into Nancy's arm. "What was that?" Bess said between clenched teeth.

"Shhhh," Nancy said. "Listen."

The clicking continued for a few seconds and then stopped.

"I think it's a mouse," Nancy said. "Or a rat. They have bigger toenails."

"Yikes! I'm outta here," Bess cried, rushing toward the door.

Nancy grabbed the Albemarle's bag, slammed the locker shut, and followed Bess out of the room.

The hallway outside the storeroom was dimly lit. Nancy held Bess back for a moment and skillfully scanned the hall, paying special attention to the corners. She saw no suspicious shadows or forms waiting for them. She quickly led Bess through the hall, up the escalator, and out the employees' door at the back of the first floor.

Safe in the parking lot, Bess let out a breath that she must have been holding since they heard those first clicks. "Nancy, this is getting weird," she said. "Someone knows that we're snooping around—and whoever it is doesn't like it."

"We'll just have to be more careful," Nancy pointed out.

Nancy drove to Scarletti's, where George and Ali were waiting for them.

"I was starting to worry about you two," George said. "Ali told me she was fired, and why. So have you two found anything?"

The four ordered pizza and sodas, and then started in on the breadsticks that were already waiting on the table. Nancy began relating what had happened since

Ali was fired. First she told them about her assault in the WAVE stockroom, and showed them the cloth she'd torn off her attacker's shirt. Then she brought out the small plastic triangle with the letter *e* and the numbers 701 on it.

"What do you suppose that is?" Ali asked. "Are you sure it belonged to the person who knocked you down?"

"It looks like a piece of a card or a badge or label of some sort," Nancy answered. "It definitely was in the person's pocket."

"Do you have any suspects yet?" George asked.

Nancy repeated what Cass's friend had told her about Diedra.

"Oh, Nancy . . . no," Ali protested. "There's no way Diedra had anything to do with stealing those dresses. I know all about how she was passed over for the job of store manager. And I know she was very disappointed. But she would never steal from the store. And she would never set me up either. She's my mentor and I trust her. She would never do anything so sneaky. It has to be someone else—someone with a better motive than that."

"Actually someone else's name did come up when I was questioning employees today," Nancy said, looking at Ali.

The young woman's cheeks flushed a pale pink.

"Me, right?" she asked. "It's about my fashion designs, I suppose."

"Fashion designs?" Bess asked. "Ali, you never mentioned anything about that."

"I've always wanted to be a designer," Ali said. "I even had several meetings with the store buyers about placing a few of my designs in WAVE on a consignment basis. I knew it was pretty unlikely, but they actually talked with me about it. They were going to make it a sort of 'pride in one of Albemarle's own employees' display." She swallowed a gulp of soda.

"But the new store manager finally decided against it," Ali continued, staring at the table. "They all were very encouraging and told me to keep at it and even get more training. But I was pretty bummed that they couldn't support me by placing my designs in the store."

"So someone figured that you're mad enough about that to lash out at the store and steal some of its most expensive stuff?" George asked.

"Of course that's not true," Ali said. "I could never do such a thing. And besides—I still have the dream of seeing my designs in the couturier rooms on the second floor. I wouldn't dare do anything to spoil that." Nancy could see tears glistening in Ali's smoky blue eyes. "Although it looks pretty spoiled now."

"It's okay, Ali," Bess said. "Nancy's going to figure this out. Aren't you?" Bess's eyebrows arched as she waited for Nancy's answer.

Nancy's instincts told her that Ali was telling the truth. "I'll definitely keep investigating," she said "Something's going on, and someone's not happy that we're looking into it and asking questions."

"Anything I can do to help?" George asked.

"We'll find something," Nancy answered. "I don't know if Wayne will need me to work with the decorators or not. But I'm planning on going in tomorrow anyway. Why don't you come in too? We can snoop around the store. No one knows you, or knows that you have any connection with Bess or me."

The four finished their supper and left Scarletti's. When Nancy got home, she found a message from Wayne Weber waiting on her answering machine. He explained that the ailing crew member would not be in the next day, and asked Nancy to report for work at nine in the morning.

As Nancy finally fell into bed that night, she rubbed the shoulder that was slammed into the WAVE stockroom wall. She fell asleep more determined than ever to get to the bottom of the case.

Friday morning, Nancy and Bess arrived early so they could report the previous day's incidents to Jack Lee. The store was very quiet at this hour. A few salespeople were chatting, but most of the employees hadn't arrived yet.

The management offices were located at the end of a long hallway in the back of the second floor. Jack Lee's office was the last one. He was sipping coffee and reading what looked like reports of some kind. "Well, well, Nancy Drew," he said, putting the papers down on his desk.

"Good morning," Nancy greeted him. "This is my friend Bess Marvin. She's working with Wayne Weber and the Special Effects holiday crew."

"You guys are doing a great job," Jack said. "Best decorations we've had in years. So what's up?"

Nancy put the Albemarle's sack on Jack's desk and told him about Bess's locker break-in. Carefully Jack removed the tattered scarf with the note still pinned to it. "This could just be some prank," he said.

"Shredding that scarf is a pretty mean prank," Nancy said. "And it doesn't explain that note."

"Why would someone want to send you and Bess a warning like this?" Jack asked, rereading the note.

Reluctantly Nancy told the detective about her exploration of the WAVE stockroom and the person who knocked her down. "I pulled off part of the attacker's shirt," she concluded, putting the navy blue scrap on the desk. "And this was inside." She placed the triangular piece of laminated paper on the cloth.

Jack's eyes narrowed when he saw the plastic triangle. *It's almost as if he recognizes that,* Nancy thought, studying his face.

"Ali Marie thinks she was fired because she is suspected of stealing the dresses from WAVE," Nancy said aloud. "Do you have any evidence that points to her?"

"Now, you know I can't really comment on that," Jack said. "That investigation is still open."

"Well, I know there have been other recent thefts from the store," Nancy said. "Do you think they have all been done by the same person? Or are we talking about isolated incidents?"

"We're looking at all the possibilities," Jack said. "If we think you can help us out, we'll let you know. Meanwhile," he said, looking down at the scarf, "it looks as if you should just drop this case and leave it to us to solve."

They were interrupted by a young man at the door. "Jack, I'm glad you're in already. There's been a call for you to come to the electronics department."

"I'll be right there," Jack said, standing up. Then he turned to Nancy and Bess. "Thanks for reporting the incidents and for bringing in these items. If you have any more problems, be sure to let me know."

He walked to the door, then waited for Nancy and Bess to follow him. He escorted them out and shut the door behind him. The three walked down the hall leading away from the management offices and back out to the sales floor. Nancy heard a couple of voices from behind closed doors, but the area seemed pretty deserted at this early hour.

Nancy watched Jack stride toward the electronics department, then she turned to Bess. "You go on down and get our decorating assignments," she said. "I want to look around here a little longer. I'll meet you in a few minutes."

"Okay," Bess said. "But be careful. You heard what he said."

Nancy lingered around the eyeglasses department, trying on several frames. In the mirror she could see Jack Lee halfway across the room, talking to a saleswoman. When he finally moved out of her vision and farther away, Nancy darted back into the hallway toward the management offices.

All of the offices were closed, and there was no one in sight. Within seconds she had slipped back inside Jack's office. She locked the door from the inside and walked straight to his desk.

She knew she didn't have much time, so she gathered up the papers Jack had been reading when she first came in. They appeared to be recent security reports. She made copies on the machine in the corner of the office. Nancy was careful to replace the pages so they looked as if they hadn't been touched.

As she rummaged around the desk, Nancy found

an ID badge with Jack's name and an Albemarle's code number on it. She found the plastic triangle she had grabbed from her attacker in the WAVE stockroom. When she held it against Jack's ID badge, the corners matched up perfectly. The *e* on the triangle matched up with the last letter in "Lee." The number on Jack's badge read 143701. On the scrap, the first digit of the number was broken off—only a bottom curve was left. The next three digits were 701.

Nancy shuddered as she realized what this could mean. *Could it actually have been Jack Lee who slammed me into the wall last night?* she wondered. *I've got to get out of here.* The faster she moved, the louder her heart seemed to pound. She made a photocopy of his badge, and of the laminated scrap she'd taken from her assailant. Then she carefully replaced everything. She felt as if she couldn't move fast enough, like she was watching herself in slow motion. She put all the photocopies she'd made in her backpack.

At the office door she quietly slipped the lock and turned the knob. The door felt heavy as she pulled it toward her. A rush of cold rippled down her back when she realized why. Standing before her, his hand on the opposite knob, was Jack Lee.

6

Jingle Bell Rock

When he first saw Nancy in his office, Jack's face registered shock. But his expression quickly changed to anger. His breath came out in short bursts. He looked like he wanted to say something, but was too furious to talk.

Nancy summoned all her courage and smiled broadly. "Hi, again," she said in a cheery voice.

"What are you doing here?" Jack's words came out slowly, with a slight pause after each one.

"I forgot my pen and came back to get it," she said, still smiling. Without being obvious, Nancy tried to size up Jack to see if he could have been the one who slammed her to the floor in the WAVE stockroom. "I'd better get to work," she said. "Trust me. Nobody in the store wants to see how Wayne gets if we're late." She stepped around Jack and started down the hall without looking back.

"Stay out of our way," he called in an ominous tone. "We don't need your help on this one."

Nancy kept walking and never turned back.

When she got to the Special Effects headquarters downstairs, Bess was waiting for her. "I didn't think you'd ever get here," she said.

Nancy filled her in on what she'd found while she put the backpack in her locker.

"Do you really think he could be the one who attacked you?" Bess asked, her eyes wide with shock.

"His size and build are right," Nancy said, slipping on her green blazer. "And the laminated fragment lines up with that part of his ID badge. He'd at least make a great in-house accomplice."

Nancy and Bess spent most of the morning on the mezzanine, helping Wayne assemble the tall canvas screens that would mask the holly tree from the eyes of onlookers. He wanted no one to see the tree as it was being decorated. He planned to remove the screens on Saturday and unveil the spectacular creation.

While they worked, Nancy spotted George in sporting goods on the first floor. She took a break so she could meet with George. First Nancy told her friend about her experience earlier that morning with Jack Lee.

"This case is really heating up," George said. "I've got all day, so put me to work."

"That's great," Nancy said. "I'd like you to hang out in the electronics department."

"That's not work for me," George said. "I love it up there."

"Talk to the employees," Nancy continued. "Tell them you heard about the thefts. See if any of them will talk about it. Find out anything you can: when they happened, how they think the thieves pulled it off, who the suspects might be. I'll come up during lunch break."

"I'm on it," George said. "See you later."

After George stepped onto the escalator, Nancy walked to a public pay phone located by the main entrance to the store. She called her father's hotel in Chicago and left a message to have him call her at home that evening.

When she returned to the mezzanine, Wayne, Bess, and Cass were securing the tree with wires. Wayne had designed special cleats at the end of the wires that attached the tree securely to the mezzanine railing and to the floor. The tree was even larger than Nancy had imagined from Bess's description. It was nearly as wide as the stairway, and the top grazed the ceiling. Nancy imagined it covered with silver-and-white decorations and twinkling lights. It would be a dazzling spectacle.

The crew unpacked and uncoiled dozens of strands of lights. Then they began the tedious job of attaching them to the tree. "This is going to take forever," Bess whispered to Nancy. "Wayne is so particular. He wants the lights to be as evenly spaced as possible, and there are thousands of them!"

"And none of the wires can show," added Cass, only she didn't whisper.

"That's right, girls," Wayne called out from the other side of the enormous tree. "This has to be absolute perfection. It will be the showpiece of the whole store."

"At least it's artificial," Bess observed, twining a strand of lights in and out of the dark green leaves. "These points are sharp enough, but the ones on real holly leaves stab like cacti."

They weren't even close to finishing the lights, but Wayne finally declared a lunch break. Bess and Cass headed toward the tearoom. Nancy stashed her green blazer behind the tree and walked down the mezzanine stairway to the first floor. Then she took the escalator up to electronics.

When she arrived, Nancy noticed George talking to a young man about DVD players. She left them alone and struck up a conversation with a woman behind the counter.

The woman looked like she was about fifty years old, and at first seemed a little suspicious of Nancy's probing questions. When Nancy took out her pen and notebook, the woman seemed to relax.

"Oh, you're going to take notes?" the woman asked. "So you're a reporter," the woman concluded. "Or are you one of the investigators?"

"I'm just gathering facts on the case," Nancy said. She bent her head toward the woman and spoke in a low voice. "Actually I'm working undercover. I'd appreciate it if you could help me out."

"Oh, I'll bet you're one of the new people they've hired on," the woman said. "I knew they'd added some security since the thefts started. We even have a full-time guard now, instead of that fellow who used to stop by now and again. Sure, I'd be glad to help you out."

"Fine. Mary—were you working when the thefts occurred?" Nancy asked, reading the woman's name off her Albemarle's nametag.

"No, they were all at night," Mary said. "We'd report to work in the morning, and stuff would be missing."

"No one could discreetly shoplift your most expensive items," Nancy pointed out. "Large-screen TV sets, elaborate sound systems, computer components—they're too large to hide under a coat." Nancy smiled at Mary, who grinned back.

"That's for sure," Mary said. "Besides, we have pretty good security measures in place for that stuff.

First of all, the boxes have tags on them that trigger alarms at the exit doors. When a customer makes a purchase, we disable the tags here. If someone tries to walk out without buying, the alarm sounds at the door."

"What if a customer tries to disable these alarm tags?" Nancy asked.

"They'll be pretty sorry if they do. The tags squirt bright magenta dye and sound alarms if they're tampered with. Only we can disable them without setting off the dye and alarms."

"I see video cameras positioned around the ceiling and walls," Nancy observed. "Are they on twenty-four hours a day?"

"They are," Mary answered.

Nancy looked around the department, noting the location of the security cameras. As she did, she saw the dark-haired woman that Ali had suspected from WAVE. Nancy remembered following the woman, but not seeing anything really suspicious about her.

"Have you seen that woman before?" Nancy asked.

Mary studied the dark-haired woman for a moment. "You know, I have. She kind of shows up, hangs around for a while, then disappears. Ooooh, you think she's the one, don't you?"

Mary glanced from Nancy to the other woman. Nancy could see that Mary was starting to enjoy the idea of helping to nab the thief. Nancy closed her notebook and put away her pen.

"Shall I help you catch her?" Mary whispered.

"No, that won't be necessary. She isn't a suspect." As Nancy looked at the dark-haired woman, the woman's head turned. She stared directly at Nancy for an instant, then turned and disappeared. *Or is she?* Nancy asked herself.

"She's getting away," Mary pointed out.

"Really, it's okay," Nancy said. "She's done nothing wrong. There's no reason to follow her."

She pulled Mary back to the subject of the electronics department thefts, but found out nothing more that would help. Nancy thanked Mary and strolled over to meet George. The two compared notes on what they had learned and found out that George hadn't picked up anything new. George agreed to keep asking questions and to meet Nancy and Bess later in the tearoom.

As Nancy started back toward the mezzanine, she saw a crowd gathering inside the front door of the store. TV cameramen were circling around, and reporters were talking to various couples in the throng. Against the wall, a trio of musicians played soft beautiful music, which was punctuated by the whistling of electric machinery. Several members of the Special Effects crew were assembling a two-story metal scaffolding.

Bess ran down the mezzanine steps to greet Nancy. "Our assignment has been changed," she said, her voice singing with excitement. "We're going to do the clock." She pointed toward the hubbub at the main entrance to the store.

"I figured that's what it was," Nancy said with a nod. She followed her friend's gaze to the enormous ornate iron clock hanging from the ceiling over the gathering crowd. "You know the tradition," Bess said, with a grin. "And this year, *we're* in charge of it!"

Nearly everyone in River Heights knew the tradition of the Albemarle's clock. Since it had first been attached to the ceiling, "I'll meet you under the clock" had become the catchphrase for people heading to downtown River Heights. Every year at this time, a huge pendant of mistletoe was hung from the bottom of the clock. Then this spot became the place to go if you wanted to get or give a kiss. Dozens of couples were already waiting to be among the first to kiss under the clock this year.

"Wayne asked if we were afraid of heights, and I told him no. He's going up with us. He said to give them another ten minutes," Bess said. "Look at the crowd. This is sooo much fun!"

Nancy laughed as Bess's spoke. By the time they worked their way through the crowd to the foot of the scaffolding, the rest of the crew was gone. Only Wayne was left.

"Oh, good," he said. "You're here. We don't want the kissing crowd to get too restless! Let's hang this mistletoe and get out of here."

Nancy felt almost like they were rock climbing. Wayne led the way. Over his shoulder he toted the large cluster of silk mistletoe, with its white berries, bells, and teal blue velvet bow. Nancy followed Wayne, and Bess was last. They climbed straight up the scaffolding, using the metal steps anchored into the sides.

When they reached the top, they could touch the enormous clock. "Whoa, it's really huge," Bess said. The clock face was at least eight feet in diameter and framed in a black iron casing of giant carved vines, flowers, and birds. It read 3:30.

"Okay, this is going to hang down from the clock like a pendant," Wayne explained as he uncoiled the mistletoe. "These three chains will fasten to the clock through those three openings." He pointed to holes created by the ornate carving. "Okay, each of us can take one of the chains, and . . . Oh, no! I can't believe it. Do I have to do absolutely *every* little thing?"

"What's the matter?" Nancy asked.

"There are only two chains here," Wayne said, shaking his head. "We have to have all three." He looked down to the floor. From their vantage point, they could see just about every section of the room.

"I don't see any of the crew," Wayne said. He

walked to the edge of the scaffolding. "Looks like I'll have to go get it," he said. "It might take me a while if I have to go all the way to the basement."

He looked at Nancy and Bess. "Are you two going to be okay up here? Do you want to go down and wait on the floor?"

"We'll be okay," Nancy said. Bess nodded her agreement.

Wayne started down the two-story structure, and Nancy and Bess sat down on the platform. While they waited, Nancy told Bess what she and George had learned from the electronics employees.

As she talked, Nancy felt a slight tremor, almost like a minor earthquake she had once felt. It came and went so quickly, she thought she might have imagined it. But the look on Bess's face told her it was real.

"What was that?" Bess asked.

"Actually it felt like a—" Nancy's words were cut off by a sudden dip in the corner of the scaffolding. A grinding metal sound whistled through the air, and the scaffolding teetered to one side. The bells attached to the mistletoe jingled as the platform rocked.

Nancy scrambled to her feet and helped Bess up. "We have to get off of this thing, Nancy," Bess said. Her face was white as she spoke. "We have to get down *now*!"

Nancy's stomach lurched as the platform rocked

again beneath her feet. Horrified, she looked down to the floor. A scream penetrated the buzz from below. The floor buckled under Nancy's feet as the corner of the scaffolding gave way. "It's too late for that!" she yelled. "Follow me! *Jump!*"

7

Not a Creature Was Stirring?

"Come on, Bess!" Nancy yelled again. "Jump!"

With a burst of adrenaline, Nancy leaped off the teetering platform and grabbed one of the large iron birds fashioned into the casing of the huge clock. Bess followed, clinging to a carved flower.

The buzz of excitement about the mistletoe changed to screams as people on the floor two stories below became aware of what was happening.

"Are you okay?" Nancy called over to Bess.

"I . . . I guess so," Bess said, her voice shaky. As she spoke, the corner of the scaffolding gave way, and the side caved in. The remaining parts of the structure barely clung together, forming a sort of giant leaning pyramid frame.

"Nancy! Bess!" Wayne's voice boomed through a

bullhorn two stories down. "Hang on! We're getting the big ladder!"

It seemed to take forever, but it was only a few minutes. Still, Nancy's fingers and shoulders were starting to tire as she clung to the black iron bird. She took her mind off her own discomfort by cheering Bess on.

The "big ladder" was a two-story stepladder with a heavy-duty brace, and it reached Nancy and Bess easily. Wayne climbed up quickly to help them down.

Bess went first. Relief washed over Nancy as she finally felt the ladder's first step under her feet. She stood there for a moment to give her knees time to stop wobbling.

Nancy and Bess were taken by Wayne and the store manager to the executives' lounge, where they were given sodas, tea, sandwiches, and muffins. After making sure that they were okay, Wayne left to finish hanging the mistletoe. The store manager hovered over Nancy and Bess for a while longer. He urged them to stay and rest as long as they needed to, then left to return to work.

When they were finally alone, Nancy turned to Bess. "That might not have been an accident," she said. "I—"

"There you are!" George's familiar voice filled the room as she walked in. Her close-cropped dark brown hair was clamped down with a baseball cap.

Under her peacoat she wore jeans and a yellow sweater.

"I've been looking all over for you," she said. "I was in the crowd under the clock. I tried to climb up the ladder to help you, but the Special Effects guy wouldn't let me. What's his name—Wayne? Then you were whisked away so fast I lost you in the crowd. I finally got some security woman to tell me where you were." She grabbed a sandwich and a soda and sat down. "What were you saying when I walked in?" she asked Nancy.

"I was saying that might not have been an accident," Nancy repeated. "Think about it. First I'm attacked in the WAVE stockroom. Then someone breaks into Bess's locker and shreds her scarf. Now this. I wish I could have checked the scaffolding. They shuffled us away so fast I didn't get a chance to examine it."

"Someone's really trying to scare us off," Bess said.

"And that means we might be on to something— or someone," Nancy said. She took a long drink of her soda. "I just don't know *who* yet."

"Could it possibly be Diedra?" George asked.

"Ali definitely doesn't think so," Bess said.

"Well, how about that strange dark-haired woman that's been hanging around?" George suggested.

"I think it could be either of them," Nancy said. "Diedra has a motive, and she sure has lots of opportunity." Nancy reached for a muffin. "We have no idea what's up with the dark-haired woman. I need to find out more about her."

"Or it might even be Jack Lee?" George offered. "That could have been part of his ID badge you pulled off of your assailant in the stockroom."

"It could be anyone else whose name ends in *e* and who has those last three ID numbers," Nancy said. "Or someone could have stolen or forged a similar badge. I'm not ready to rule Jack out. But we don't really have a motive for him at this point."

"Hey, easy money is a pretty good motive," George pointed out.

"You're right," Nancy agreed. "The main thing is that there is some connection between the person who knocked me down and Albemarle's security badges."

"Well, if it is Jack or some other security person, they sure know the best time to take stuff and how to disable the alarms," Bess added.

"Exactly," Nancy said. Deep down, she hoped she was wrong in suspecting Jack. She'd worked well with police, detectives, and security guards on past cases and always respected their courage. She would hate to find out that there was a bad apple in the barrel. But she also knew that if there was one, she needed to find it.

"So what's next?" George said.

"Being one of the decorators has been great, because it has given me more access to the store. But I haven't had any time to look around, except on my breaks and during lunch hours."

"What are you getting at?" George asked.

"We need to stay after hours, after everyone leaves. I want to check out the electronics department stockroom and some other places. And I want to get into Albemarle's employee database."

"You know you can count on me for that," Bess assured her. Bess was a skilled computer hacker.

"Okay," Nancy said, standing up. "How about tonight? You both okay with that?"

"It's good for me," George said. "I've got some errands to run, but I can be back by eight."

Nancy checked her watch. It was 4:35. She told George to meet them at 8:30 in the sporting goods department, and George left.

Bess and Nancy checked in with Wayne on the first floor beneath the clock. He told them that the scaffolding had been fixed—some screws at the bottom of one corner had broken. They all looked up at the mistletoe, but no one spoke. Finally Wayne broke the silence.

"You're probably sore from hanging up there," he said. "So I want you to take it easy the rest of the day. I'll need your strength tomorrow evening." He took them down to the storeroom and showed them cartons of mistletoe garlands and boxes of ivory ribbon. He showed them how he wanted them to weave the two together, and then he left.

Nancy and Bess worked until 8:30, when Nancy left to meet George. Nancy led her friend down to the storeroom.

It was around a quarter to nine when they heard decorators coming down the hall. Nancy shuffled Bess and George to the back of the storeroom. The three hid underneath the wraps that covered the mechanical figures, while the other crew members gathered their belongings to leave for the night. Finally Nancy heard the light switch click and the door close. It was very quiet.

"Wait a few more minutes," Nancy whispered. "We want to make sure no one is coming back." After a few moments Nancy gave the signal and carefully pulled back her cover. The room was dark. She turned on her penlight, shielding it with her hand until she was positive they were alone. She walked quickly to the door and put her ear against it.

"I don't hear anyone out in the hall," she told the others. Then she flicked on the lights. The room glowed with that harsh fluorescent yellow light.

"I couldn't have stayed still under that drape much longer," George said. "That freaky mechanical dog had his nose on the back of my neck."

"You're lucky," Bess said. "I was sitting next to the

little girl. Every time I let out a breath, feathers blew off her hat. I almost sneezed twice."

"Okay, let's get out of here," Nancy said. "Remember, there's a guard on duty, and we don't know where he'll be. I know where the security cameras are—we have to dodge them, so follow my lead."

They stepped quietly down the basement hall, which was lit by greenish globes near the ceiling. "We can't use the elevator because of the noise," Nancy whispered. "We'll take the stairs."

Nancy's senses were on full alert as they walked up the steps and through the door to the second floor. The large chandeliers were turned off. Some of the display cases had small lights under the glass, but most of them were dark. A few bulbs along the walls streaked a pale blue shadow over the floor. Sprinkled throughout the room, mannequins appeared like gray ghosts in odd poses.

"Oooooh, I'm not sure I like this place at night," Bess said. "It's really spooky."

"Come on," Nancy urged. "The guard doesn't seem to be anywhere around."

She led Bess and George to the human resources office, where the employee records were kept. With just a few twists of her lock pick, they were in. George stood by the door, keeping watch over the hall, while Bess booted up the computer at the front desk.

"Go straight to the security files," Nancy told Bess as she produced a piece of paper from her pocket. "Here's Jack Lee's password—I found it written on a scrap of paper in his desk drawer this morning."

While Bess clicked away, Nancy checked the file cabinets. The only lights in the room were Nancy's penlight beam and the green glow of the computer screen.

Nancy pulled a file up out of the drawer and opened it. "I found Diedra Haize," she whispered to the others. Scanning it, she called out her report. "Triple-A rating, lots of wonderful recommendations from managers here and from another store she worked for in St. Paul. There's even a memo here from Albemarle's former store manager. He recommended her for the job and says she should never have been passed over. He's urging the store to promote her."

"See, Ali was right," Bess said. "Okay, I've got the security personnel list here. What do you want to know?"

Nancy refiled Diedra's folder and joined Bess at the desk. The computer listed a small security staff: Jack, three full-time and two part-time associates, and the new night guard.

"We've got a work history and a background check on each one," Nancy said, "plus a description." She read through each employee's data as Bess clicked the pages down. "Whoa, here's something," Nancy said, when she reached the end of the file. "There's a memo that says because of recent shrinkage, Quality Control Facilitator Herbe will put in extra hours and serve as undercover security representative, to be paid seventy-five percent by corporate and twenty-five percent by security."

"She wasn't in the security file," Bess said.

"Try 'quality control,'" Nancy suggested.

Bess searched under that label and brought up a new list of names. She scrolled down to "Herbe."

"'Diana Herbe,'" Nancy read aloud, "'undercover representative to monitor department supervisors and managers and assess their work habits and skills. Loaned to security.'"

Nancy thought for a minute, then shared her idea. "If this Diana Herbe is working for security now, she's going to do more than check out employee work habits. I'll bet she's supposed to discover whether they're thieves. What does she look like?"

Bess read the physical description. It matched perfectly with the dark-haired woman whom Ali had suspected and Nancy had followed.

"What's her employee ID number?" Nancy asked.

"It's 218701," Bess said.

"That would match the scrap I took from my attacker," Nancy said. "Maybe she's using her new position as a launching pad for her own—"

"Shhhh," George hissed from the door. "I heard something in the hall."

Nancy motioned for everyone to hide. She and George stepped to the end of the row of file cabinets and leaned back out of sight. Bess turned off the computer monitor and ducked down behind the desk.

The hairs on the back of Nancy's neck fluttered as she heard footsteps approaching the office. The sound grew louder, then passed by the door and faded away a little. Then the footsteps stopped and started back toward the office. Whoever was in the hall stopped outside the door.

Nancy held her breath.

Finally the person walked away, and this time there was no return visit.

Nancy stepped out from her hiding spot, and George followed. Bess closed down the computer before joining them at the door. Nancy listened carefully, but heard nothing from the hallway. She slowly turned the knob and opened the door.

"I think we're clear," she whispered, "but we've got to be careful. If that was the guard, he's probably continued on his rounds, and we have some time. But if it *wasn't* the guard, then we could be in trouble."

"Where do we go next?" Bess whispered. Nancy could tell from the tone of her voice that she was feeling a little shaky.

"I want to check out the electronics department stockroom," Nancy said, her voice still a whisper. "It's at the other end of this floor."

"What was that?" Bess said, her hand gripping Nancy's arm. "Someone's still out there."

Nancy strained to hear. She heard a shuffling noise against the carpet and the faint plastic rattling of hangers bobbing against each other. It sounded like someone was moving through racks of clothes.

Nancy gestured for the three to separate and take cover. She circled around the racks until she found a large cardboard sign announcing a special display of wind suits. The sign was a perfect screen. Nancy stepped behind it. In the distance she could hear a tumbling, rolling sound.

After a few minutes, the department was very still again. Cautiously Nancy crept from behind the sign and took a few tentative steps. As she crept along in the pale bluish light, she strained her ears to hear every sound. But she wasn't prepared for the feeble cry that filtered through the shirts and sweaters: "Nancy . . . I'm . . . help me!"

8

Cornered

"Nancy . . . help!"

Nancy heard the familiar voice again. It was George, and she was clearly in pain.

"George, where are you?" Nancy called.

"Escalator," George responded, her voice weak. "First floor . . . bottom."

"Nancy! There you are," Bess cried, running through two racks of workout pants. "Where's George?"

"Here . . . down here," George called out.

"She's at the bottom of the escalator," Nancy said, leading Bess toward the rumbling sound of the moving staircase. When they reached it, they saw George's crumpled body lying at the foot of the escalator.

"George!" Bess cried.

"We're coming," Nancy said, jumping on to the steps. She and Bess raced down the staircase, not willing to ride down slowly.

"What happened?" Nancy asked when she reached George, gently probing her friend's arms and legs for possible injuries.

"I'm okay, except for my leg," George answered. She reached down and moved her leg with her hands so it wasn't in such an awkward position. Nancy could tell by the grimace on George's face that it hurt to move her leg even a couple of inches.

"When you motioned for us to take cover, I moved out to find a hiding place. Just as I passed the escalator, someone came out of nowhere and gave me a major shove. I fell backward onto the escalator. There was no way I could get my footing while it moved, so I just tumbled on down to the bottom."

Nancy scanned around the room and back up the escalator. "Whoever it was is nowhere in sight now," she said. "We need to get you to the hospital. Besides, I'd like to get out of here before the night guard catches us. Can you walk?"

"I don't think so," George said, cradling her knee.

"Don't move," Nancy said. "I'll be right back."

Keeping low and watching for anyone else who might be walking around the first floor, Nancy headed across the room. When she arrived at sporting goods, she grabbed a rubber raft from a large display. Then she tore back to where George and Bess were waiting.

Carefully Nancy and Bess rolled George from the floor over into the middle of the raft. Then, using the raft as a gurney, they dragged it to the employees' door at the back of the store. They pulled the raft with George lying on it to a hidden spot behind a stand of silk trees—just inside the door. Bess stayed with George while Nancy went down to Special Effects headquarters.

Nancy tiptoed down the exit stairs, still listening for any suspicious sounds. When she reached the basement, she opened the door just a few inches. When she saw and heard nothing, she raced down the hall to the storeroom.

Inside the room she headed straight for her locker. She grabbed her coat and backpack, and went to Bess's locker and took her coat and purse. Then she ran out of the room, down the hall, and up the steps to rejoin Bess and George.

Nancy and Bess tore across the parking lot, pulling George in the rubber raft. When they got to the car, they hoisted their friend up into the backseat so she could stretch out her leg. Nancy deflated the raft and threw it in her trunk. Then she drove to the River Heights Hospital emergency room.

Nancy and Bess sat in the ER waiting room while George was being examined. "Nancy, I'm really scared," Bess said. "George could have been hurt really badly."

"And whoever pushed her didn't care," Nancy added. "But we have a possible new clue, Bess. We might have an ID for the woman who's been hanging around the store. If she's just doing her job, she has every right to hang around. But if it was the corner of *her* security badge that I pulled off when I was attacked, then we have a real lead."

"But how do we find out for sure?" Bess asked.

"I contacted my father and asked him to check out Jack Lee. If he's okay, I'll tell him about our new findings. If he's not, I'll probably go to the police."

At last the doctor wheeled George out from the examining room. Her leg was encased in a walking cast and propped up on the wheelchair leg rest. She looked a little pale and shaky, but she grinned at Nancy and Bess.

"All the X rays are clear," the doctor told them. "No breaks. But she's sprained that knee pretty badly. She can go home, but she needs to take it easy for a few days and then have it checked again."

Nancy drove Bess and George home. By the time she got to her room and showered, it was 11:30. She checked the message on her answering machine. The rich, welcome voice of her father sang out into the room.

"Hi, honey," Carson Drew said. "I had some associates check out Jack Lee. He seems to be legitimate and highly regarded. It sounds as if you can trust him. Just be careful. Things are going pretty well here. I'll be home Sunday."

"I was hoping you'd say that," Nancy said to the voice on the answering machine. "See you soon." She emptied her backpack onto her desk and laid out the photocopies she had made in Jack's office that morning. On the left, she placed the copy of the triangular scrap of plastic she had wrested from her attacker in the WAVE stockroom. On the right, she lined up the photocopy of Jack's ID card.

She measured Jack's card. Then, using it as a guide, she diagrammed a duplicate ID card, filling in the name and ID number of "Diana Herbe," the quality-control facilitator they had found in security's employee database, and 218701. She placed the copy of the laminated triangle over her drawing. The *e* of "Herbe" and the 701 of Diana's ID number matched up perfectly.

Nancy finally fell into bed. "Maybe we finally have a break in this case," she mumbled as she fell asleep.

Saturday morning, Nancy called George and found out she was feeling okay. Then she picked up Bess and drove to Albemarle's.

"Thanks for coming early this morning," Nancy said. "No problem," Bess said. "We don't have to be there till ten o'clock anyway. It'll give me a chance to check out some new shoes. I need some sandals to go with my new holiday dress."

"I'm going straight to Jack Lee's office. I'll come get you if he needs to talk to you, too."

"You're not going to tell him we were in the personnel office, are you? Or that we hacked into the computer?" Bess asked.

"Not if I can help it," Nancy said.

Jack wasn't in his office, so Nancy had him paged. He was there in a few minutes.

"So you and your friend had quite an adventure yesterday, I hear," Jack said.

Nancy's mind spun into defense mode. *How did he find out we were here after hours last night?* she thought. Then her keen instincts jumped in. *No one saw us but the person who pushed George down the escalator. He's talking about the scaffolding, I'll bet.* Seconds later, he confirmed this.

"Those temporary scaffolding structures can be pretty tricky to assemble," he said. "Sounds like that one was made in a hurry."

"Did any of your security people take a look at it after it collapsed?" Nancy asked. "I'm not sure it was an accident," Nancy said, "but I can't prove that it wasn't."

"What do you mean?" Jack sat down behind his

76

desk, and gestured for Nancy to take the seat opposite him.

She began by reminding him of her encounter in the WAVE stockroom and the threat in Bess's locker. Then she told him about staking out the store the previous night, and George's assault.

Jack's large brown eyes narrowed as he listened to Nancy. Then he leaned forward, his elbows resting on the desk. "I asked you not to meddle in this case, Nancy. But in a way I'm glad you did—and I respect your opinion. So who do you think is doing all this?" he asked. "And why?"

"I think it's connected to the thefts you've been having here lately," she answered. "As you know, Ali and Bess are good friends. As a favor to them, I did a little investigating and asked some questions. It looks like someone's trying to throw me off the case."

"I see," Jack said. He looked at her intently.

Nancy couldn't tell whether he believed her or not. She was determined to make him understand. If he was the top-notch detective that her father's associates maintained he was, he could be an important ally in clearing Ali's name.

"Someone I know was able to hack into some of Albemarle's computer records," she began, "and—"

"What?!" Jack exploded. "Who?"

"I'd rather not reveal my source," Nancy answered.

"You have to trust me on this. Nothing was done to the records. You have my word that no use will be made of them except what I tell you here, and it will not happen again."

"I'll let it go for now," Jack said. "But I warn you—if anything happens because of it, you and the hacker will be in real trouble."

"That's fair. Now let me tell you what we found out. Do you know Diana Herbe?"

"If you got into the database, you probably know that I do," Jack said. "She's been working part-time for us since the thefts began."

Nancy reminded him of the woman she had suspected of shoplifting. She pointed out that Diana's description fit that woman and also could have been the person who knocked her down in the WAVE stockroom.

"Well, the first connection is plausible," Jack said. "Of course, Diana Herbe is going to be hanging around. That's her job. And you said you didn't see the person who attacked you. You don't even know whether it was a man or a woman."

"But I did get something that belonged to that person, remember?" Nancy said. She pulled out the photocopy of the laminated triangle scrap. "These numbers are the same as the last ones in her ID number."

Jack reached into his desk and took out the actual

fragment. He studied it for a moment, and then pushed the intercom button on his desk. His assistant's voice answered. "Page Diana Herbe, please. Ask her to come here immediately."

He turned to Nancy. "I checked all of security's badges, but I didn't check the ones in quality control."

The minute the woman walked in and saw Nancy, her cheeks began to flush a purplish red. Jack introduced the two. Diana just nodded to Nancy.

"May I see your security card, Diana?" Jack asked.

"Well . . . it's . . . um . . . it's in my other jacket," Diana stammered. She began to back up to the door. "I'll go get it and be right back."

"Diana," Jack said, in a commanding voice. The woman stopped in her tracks. "Diana," Jack said in a gentler tone, "give me your ID card."

Diana's head went up and her shoulders seemed very stiff. Her cheeks turned an even darker purple.

She plunged her hand deep into her pocket. She pulled out a plastic card and smacked it down on Jack's desk. The upper-right corner was missing.

9

Boughs Away!

Without a word, Jack picked up the small triangle that Nancy had torn from her attacker and showed it to Diana. Then he fitted it to the broken corner of her card. It meshed perfectly.

Diana looked from Jack to Nancy, then back to Jack. "This is my *job,* Jack," she said. "I had every right to be in that stockroom in WAVE. Every right to be anywhere in this store. I'm *supposed* to be testing the store, its employees, and its security policies. And also to help nail the thief."

"Does that include knocking me into the wall?" Nancy asked.

"How did I know who you were?" Diana challenged. "I'm supposed to be undercover here. I need to keep my identity secret. You could have been the thief. We'd just had some dresses taken from that department, after all. Or you could have been someone Jack had hired to follow me, to monitor my actions. Is that what's going on here, Jack?"

She glared at him, and her voice took on a sort of snarly sound. "You've been after me since I first joined the security team. What's the matter, Jack? Was I too good? Were you afraid I might crack the case before you did? Or maybe it's been you behind the thefts all this time. Was I getting too close to your little scam, Jack? Is that why you wanted me out?"

"Now you're being ridiculous," Jack said. "And you know it. I warned you once, Diana, and gave you a second chance. You blew it. Why don't you just tell us what's been going on now. The store will be a lot easier on you if you're honest."

Diana gasped as if she was going to let loose another round of accusations. And then her defiance seemed to just fade in front of Nancy's eyes. Slowly Diana's shoulders slumped and she crumpled into a chair. She took a deep breath and released it with a long sigh. Then she smiled sweetly at Nancy and Jack. It was like seeing a new person in the chair.

"Okay, okay," Diana said. "So I took the dresses. But I was just doing it to see if it could be done. Honest. I was just doing my job. I wanted to see if an ordinary customer could overcome the security and get away with it. And I did."

"And you were going to report this to me . . . when?" Jack asked.

"Eventually," Diana said. "Of course I was going to. And before you ask—I *swear* I had nothing to do with the thefts in the electronics department. Only the dresses."

"And what about attacking me in the stockroom?" Nancy asked.

"Now, I didn't really attack you, Miss Drew," Diana said. "I needed to get out of there before my cover was blown. I merely pushed you aside so I could escape discovery. I'm so sorry if you lost your balance and fell. I hope you weren't hurt." She managed one of the best fake smiles that Nancy had ever seen.

"Were you the one who tried to break into my car Wednesday night?" Nancy asked. "And left part of the lock pick in the lock?"

Diana looked at her hands, clasped in her lap. "Yes. I was going to leave a note for you to try to get you to stop following me. I saw you watching me in WAVE and then saw you follow me to the shoe department. I thought then that you might be one of Jack's operatives, spying on me. I was just trying to protect myself."

"Did you break into a locker in the Special Effects room and leave a threatening message for Bess Marvin?" Jack asked.

"Who?" Diana asked in return. "I don't know anyone by that name and didn't break into any lockers."

"What do you know about the scaffolding collapsing yesterday, with Nancy on top of it?" Jack asked.

"I heard about . . . wait a minute," Diana asked, shaking her head. "You're not saying I had anything to do with that! Come on, Jack . . . those girls could have been killed. I wouldn't have anything to do with something like that!"

"Were you in the store last night?" Nancy asked. "After hours?" She wondered if Diana could have been the one who pushed George down the escalator.

"No, why?" Diana responded.

"You're positive you weren't here?" Jack repeated Nancy's query.

"Absolutely not," Diana said. "I have a witness who can verify that."

Jack didn't respond, but went instead to his assistant's office and spoke to her in a voice too low for Nancy to hear.

Nancy and Jack interrogated Diana for a few more minutes, but she stood by her story. She had tried to break into Nancy's car and she had knocked Nancy down in the stockroom, but both incidents were in self defense. She had also stolen the dresses, but only as a test of Albemarle's security. She insisted she had nothing to do with any of the other incidents.

At last there was a knock on the door, and the

assistant showed two men into the office. Jack introduced them as River Heights police detectives, who had arrived to arrest Diana. Jack told them she was suspected in all the thefts in the store and all the attacks and threats of the past several days.

"I can't believe this, Jack," Diana raged as one of the detectives read her rights to her. "I did it as a test of the system. I told you that. You're behind the electronics thefts, aren't you? And she's probably in on the whole thing with you," she added, nodding toward Nancy. "You think by accusing me, you'll get away with it all. Well, not after I'm through. By the time I'm finished, you'll both get just what you deserve."

Diana was still muttering as the detectives escorted her out of the room.

"Well, Nancy, it looks as if you solved this case after all," Jack said, reaching out to shake her hand. "I—and Albemarle's—am deeply in your debt. It will take us a while to come up with a good way to show our appreciation, but we will—believe me."

"There's no need for any reward. But you're absolutely sure that she's responsible for all of it, everything that's happened?" Nancy asked.

"I am," Jack said, walking Nancy to the door. "Definitely. She's got all the security passwords, keys to all the equipment, knowledge of all the security disabling procedures. I won't be surprised if she has an accomplice, too—that's probably the so-called witness who'll give her an alibi for last night. I'm sure that once we wrap up our investigation and the city police finish theirs, she will be implicated in everything. Meanwhile you can start relaxing and won't need to look over your shoulder any longer."

Nancy cocked an eyebrow and looked at Jack's proud face. Something didn't seem quite right about this story, but it was probably better not to rock the boat too much right now. Nancy turned toward the door, but suddenly stopped herself.

"Wait—what about Ali?" she asked. "She's fully cleared of the WAVE thefts, right?"

"Absolutely."

"Then how soon can she have an apology and her job back?" Nancy asked. "She's been really devastated by this whole thing. I'd like to tell her that it's over."

"By all means, tell her," Jack said. "I'll tell Diedra what's happened and get Ali back onboard immediately."

"Great. Keep me posted on what turns up with the Herbe investigation."

"I promise," Jack said. "And thanks again."

Nancy hurried to the decorating crew headquarters and ran straight to Bess to give her the good news.

"Oh, Nancy, that's wonderful," Bess said, her eyes

twinkling with delight. "Let's call Ali right now."

"I'd better check in with Wayne first," Nancy pointed out. "It's almost eleven o'clock."

"Oh, Brad's back—the one who was sick," Bess said. "So you probably won't have to work today. Most of us are working down here on the mechanical figures today, anyway. We've got a lot of cleaning and repair to do. But Wayne might want you tonight. Check with him."

"What's tonight?" Nancy asked.

"We're going to the Albemarle mansion to finish up the decorating there. The family's coming home tomorrow, and there's still a bunch of stuff to do."

"That sounds like fun," Nancy said.

"Nancy? Oh, I'm glad you're here," Cass said, coming up to join them. "Wayne told me that if you showed up to ask you if you can work tonight at the Albemarles'."

"Bess already told me about it, and I'd love to."

"Super," Cass said. "I'll tell him. And Bess can fill you in on the details—when we'll start and all that."

Cass left, and Nancy and Bess called George first to update her. They were both relieved to hear that George was doing really well. She was already walking with the cast and doing the exercises that the rehab people had shown her in the hospital.

Then Nancy called Ali.

"Oh, I'm so glad you called," Ali said. She sounded

thrilled about the exciting news. "Jack and Diedra both called. I'm going back to work at WAVE tomorrow. Jack told me what you did, Nancy. You're the absolute best. And I knew I was right about Diedra. She couldn't have been involved. I'm coming right over to get reinstated and I'm meeting Diedra for a late lunch. Can you meet us there in a couple of hours?"

Bess nodded that she could make it, and Nancy told Ali they'd both be there.

When they got off the phone, they joined other Special Effects crew members who were cleaning and repairing the mechanical figures. By 12:30 all the cleaning was done, and the crew dispersed for lunch.

"We never got our present from Ali," Bess said, as she and Nancy took the escalator up to the first floor. "Remember? She said she left us something at the Millennium counter."

"Will you pick it up for us?" Nancy asked. "I forgot to give Jack the raft that we borrowed last night from sporting goods. It's pretty beaten up from being dragged through the parking lot, but I'd still like to return it. It's still in the car. I'll take that on up to him and then meet you all in the tearoom."

Jack wasn't in his office, so Nancy gave the raft and a note of explanation to his assistant. Then she went down the escalator to the first floor. The minute she stepped off the escalator, she knew something was different. There was a warm glow over the whole room and a buzz in the crowd. Everyone was looking up to the mezzanine, where the canvas screens no longer hid Wayne's masterpiece at the top of the stairs.

The enormous holly tree had been unveiled at last, and it was nearly as wide as the stairway itself. Dazzling and dramatic, it almost blinded Nancy when she gazed straight at it. Thousands of white bulbs twinkled. Hundreds of white, silver, mirrored glass ornaments shimmered in the glow. It was almost like looking at the sun it was so bright.

Nancy stared at the tree as she walked up the mezzanine steps. A ball covered with small mirrors seemed to spin on its own. One of the snowflake ornaments danced on its invisible cord, as if it were actually falling from the sky.

The first scream behind her jolted Nancy out of her trance. When she heard the second scream, she looked back. Then she followed the screamer's gaze around and up the steps.

The horror rose in her like a flare, flooding her skin with hot sparks. The tree was slowly falling toward her like a giant, glass-covered, shooting star.

10

Empty Promises

The tree was coming at her fast, and Nancy's brain and body went into overdrive. Her first instinct was to protect her eyes, and her second was to get out of the way. She turned her head away from the tumbling tree and vaulted over the iron banister onto the floor below. She could feel the swish of holly leaves graze her back as the tree skidded across the step where she'd stood.

The monster tree landed at the foot of the stairs with a cacophonous crash, spraying glass shards in all directions.

Nancy jumped up from her protective crouch at the side of the stairway. She saw Bess, Cass, Ali, and Diedra at the top of the stairs outside the tearoom. "Keep everyone back," she called to Bess. "There's glass all over the steps."

Nancy walked around to the foot of the stairs where the tree landed. Wayne Weber's masterpiece lay on its side like a spiky green-and-silver prehistoric creature. Many people nearby had apparently been so transfixed by the sight of the falling tree that they had been unable to move away in time to avoid being injured. Spikes of glass and spatters of blood were everywhere.

Jack Lee raced to Nancy. "What happened?!" he yelled. It was hard to hear over the sounds of voices calling out for their companions, shrieking into cell phones, crying in pain, and moaning for help. The chaos was almost overwhelming.

"The tree fell down the stairs," Nancy said simply.

She and Jack helped a few shoppers with medical credentials to set up a triage area until the emergency medical technicians arrived. In the triage they assessed each person's injury and ranked it in order of worst to least. Then, when the ambulance crews arrived, they would easily be able to treat the people with the most serious injuries first.

One of the doctors who had set up the triage insisted on giving Nancy a quick look. She was pronounced physically okay. Still feeling a little shaken, she worked with the triage. She helped make injured shoppers and sales clerks comfortable while they waited for medical assistance. She soothed crying children who had a parent that was injured. And she helped shoppers who had been separated by the chaos find each other again.

Jack and the other security personnel roped off an area that equaled about half of the large room. Maintenance men and women began the enormous job of sweeping tiny glass shards off of countertops and wiping blood from display cases. Sales clerks gathered up ruined merchandise and dumped it into large plastic Albemarle's bags.

"Oh, no, it can't be. . . . It's a disaster. . . . The poor people . . . my beautiful tree . . . I can't believe it!" Wayne ran up to Nancy. "I'll get help," he said, and ran off again. Within minutes, the decorators assembled to help take the tree apart and clean up the mess.

The EMTs arrived quickly and began treating the injured people and taking them to the hospital. Nancy noticed that Jack was given a message by one of his associates. He read the note, then wadded it up and jammed it into his pocket. Nancy could tell by his expression that he was angry, so she joined him.

"Bad news?" she asked.

"More shrinkage," he muttered. "The electronics department has been hit again."

"Today?" Nancy asked "This morning?"

"Not sure," Jack answered. "They're checking the inventory now. We should know more later."

"Is Diana still in jail?"

Jack nodded briefly and stomped off.

Nancy watched him go, her thoughts racing. *Diana insisted she stole only the dresses from WAVE, and not any of the other merchandise. But if Jack's right and she's involved in all of it—including this recent one—she had to have an accomplice.*

"Oh, Nancy, are you all right?" Bess's sweet voice startled Nancy out of her thoughts. She and the others had finally been able to work their way down the mezzanine steps.

"I'm fine," Nancy said. "Are you all okay? Did any of the ornaments or glass end up on the mezzanine?"

"Some," Ali said. "What a mess. Were there many people hurt?"

"A couple of dozen," Nancy answered. "Most of them were minor, but a few were pretty serious. I'm just so glad it wasn't any worse."

"Wayne's gone absolutely nuts," Bess reported. "I tried to talk to him, but he barely made sense. He's probably in some kind of shock."

"I can't imagine what all this is going to cost in damages and repairs," Ali said. "The store has lost a lot of merchandise and display cases."

"Not to mention bad publicity," Cass added. "Well, I'd better get to work. We've got a lot of cleanup to do."

"Me too," Bess said.

"Where's Diedra?" Nancy asked. "I thought I saw her up there with you."

"She was," Bess said. "She went back up to WAVE."

"She probably went to talk to her sales gang," Ali said. "This kind of accident can hit the employees really hard. Diedra's a really good manager. She'll want to make sure all her people are okay and everything. I think I'll go on up and help her. Might as well get back on the payroll today instead of waiting till tomorrow."

Ali walked to the escalator and Bess turned back to Nancy. "How about you?" she asked. "Are you sure you're okay? It was so scary, Nancy. That tree was headed straight for you."

"I'm fine, really," Nancy said. "Tell Wayne I'll be back to help clean up in a little while."

"Okay. I don't know what's happening with the schedule now with this mess. . . . We may be here all night. I'll find out by the time you get back."

Nancy left the main floor and took the escalator up to the electronics department on the second floor.

"Oh, hi—I'm glad you're here." The woman behind one of the electronics counters called out. Nancy remembered the woman's name was Mary—she was the one Nancy had questioned the day before. "Maybe you can fill us in on what happened down there." It was clear that she still believed that Nancy was working undercover for Jack.

"It was pretty wild," Nancy said. "The big tree fell over. Unfortunately, several people got hurt."

"I heard the ambulances," Mary said. "But I couldn't really leave the department. I'm going down on my break to check it out."

"Jack told me your department has suffered more shrinkage," Nancy said.

"Yes, things were taken from the stockroom and from one of the displays."

"Did it happen during the accident downstairs by any chance?" Nancy asked. "Do you think maybe it was shoplifters taking advantage of the commotion?"

"I don't think so, but I'm not sure. I just started work a half hour ago. The guy on the early shift said he thought it happened last night."

Could it have been the person who knocked George down the escalator? Nancy wondered. *The robbery could have happened while we were here in the store.*

She leaned in toward Mary. "Is anyone in the stockroom right now?" she asked in a low voice.

Mary looked around the department. "No," she whispered back. "It looks like everyone is on the floor. Why?"

"I want to go check it out," Nancy answered. "But

I don't want to blow my cover. Can you just keep everyone occupied out here for a while? I want to look around by myself."

"Sure," Mary said. "I'd be glad to help you out. If anyone even looks like they're going in there, I'll head 'em off."

"Thanks, Mary." Nancy easily slipped into the stockroom without the other employees noticing her. The layout of the room was similar to the one at WAVE, except there were no racks of clothing. Instead, open, empty boxes were scattered around the floor in sloppy piles. "These are probably boxes for the items that are on display on the sales floor," Nancy whispered to herself.

Sealed boxes of expensive electronics equipment lined two walls. The boxes were stacked from floor to ceiling, three layers deep.

As Nancy poked around behind the first stack of boxes, she noticed an odd spattering of color on the floor around and beneath some of the boxes. A trail of magenta spots led her back to those stacks closest to the walls.

She reached out to move some of the boxes in the last stack so she could follow the magenta trail. The box on the top of the stack, which was labeled as a computer tower, started to fall. Nancy braced herself to catch it. The box landed safely in her arms, but she knew instantly by its weight that it was empty.

Carefully she moved a few more boxes in the stacks closest to the walls. All the boxes were sealed and stapled shut. They looked as if they had just arrived from the factory— but they were all empty.

11

The Jigsaw Jumble

Nancy checked dozens of boxes of electronics equipment in the stockroom. The ones in the front stacks were heavy. They obviously contained what the bright-colored pictures on the outside of the boxes said they did. But several sealed, stapled boxes in the stacks along the wall were empty.

Nancy remembered her initial investigation of this department. Mary had told her that when someone tampered with some of the boxes, the security tags squirted magenta dye. *Just like these spots*, Nancy thought. She kneeled to touch the purple spots on the floor. *I'll bet that's what this is*, she concluded. *Someone has ripped off the boxes in the stacks in the back, and no one even realizes it yet.*

She restacked the boxes toward the back, leaving

them exactly as she'd found them. Then she pulled the other stacks back the way they were. She could no longer see the empty boxes. They were completely hidden by the ones in the front stacks.

She went back out to the sales floor and over to Mary, who was stacking DVD players in a display.

"Did you find anything?" Mary whispered.

"Everything's fine," Nancy said. "I'm going to leave now. I don't want to tip myself off to any of your coworkers."

"Don't worry—I'll keep your secret." Mary gave her a broad smile and went back to work.

Nancy hurried to Jack Lee's office and told him what she'd discovered. She took him back to the stockroom and showed him the empty sealed boxes.

"Unbelievable!" Jack said. "This thing is much bigger than we thought! The Albemarle family's coming back tomorrow night. Now not only do I have to tell them that we've had an accident with multiple injuries—a total public relations disaster—but I also have to reveal that the shrinkage is about triple what I'd initially reported to them."

Jack steered Nancy out of the stockroom. "I've got to get someone up here to find out just how bad the shrinkage is. I appreciate what you've done, Nancy, but I insist that you let me take it from here. This is a much bigger operation than we thought, and I don't want you to get hurt." He gave her a thin smile and stormed off.

By the time Nancy got back to the first floor, the cleanup was well underway. Nancy guessed the area around the tree would be roped off for at least the rest of the day. Cracked display cases had to be removed and merchandise restocked. It was almost as if a small car had plowed into the store.

Nancy found Bess helping to dismantle the rest of the tree. "Oh, good, you're back," Bess said. "I called George during my break and told her what happened."

"How's she doing?" Nancy asked.

"Physically, she's fine," Bess answered. "But she's pretty miserable about being tied down by that cast. She hates being left out of the action."

"We'd all like to have missed this last action, though," Nancy said, looking around.

"Anyway, the Special Effects crew is still going to the mansion after hours to finish the decorating there—no matter what's going on here. Wayne says we have to get it done before the Albemarle family comes home tomorrow. He feels like at least their home should be perfect. And it's going to be a while before the store is back to normal. So I thought we could stop by George's house before we go—maybe take her some dinner."

"Okay, I'm in," Nancy said. As she stood at the foot of the mezzanine steps, she looked up at where the tree had stood before its perilous plunge. "I'd love to see the Albemarle place." She thought back to when she, Bess, and Wayne were working on the holly tree.

"What is it?" Bess asked. "You're miles away."

"Not miles, just steps." She walked toward the stairway. "Remember yesterday when we were working with Wayne on the holly tree? We helped him secure it to the floor and to the mezzanine railing."

"Right." Bess nodded.

"Wayne designed special cleats to insure that the tree wouldn't move, to guarantee that it would be safe. A lot of people walk around up there, with the tearoom and all. He wanted to make sure there was no danger."

"Sure," Bess said. "This holly tree was his masterpiece. When I first started working for him, he talked about it a lot, about how it was his most spectacular design. He said he took a long time planning every detail of the decorating, and creating those cleats to make the tree totally secure."

"Then why did it fall?" Nancy asked. "Why did the cleats fail?" Nancy looked around. "Have you seen any of the cleats in this mess?"

"No," Bess said. "Not one."

"Look for them," Nancy said, starting up the steps. "I'll be right back."

When Nancy got to the top step, she went immediately to the spot where the holly tree had been secured. First she ran her hand along the black wrought-iron balcony railing that bordered the mezzanine. "The cleats were fastened right here," she reminded herself.

She found three small scratches in the black wrought-iron paint where the steel cleats had been attached. But other than that, there was no sign the tree had ever been secured to the railing.

Then she examined the floor. The six large brass eyebolts were still there. They were very long, thick screws with circles of brass sticking up on top. Wayne had used a machine to anchor them deep into the floor. Then he had strung six wires down from the tree. His special cleats attached the wire to the eyebolts in the floor.

She pulled on the eyebolts with all her strength. They didn't move at all—they were still firmly anchored. She ran her fingers along the floor around the eyebolts, but didn't draw even a tiny splinter. *There's no sign that tree was wrenched away from these bolts with enough force to shoot down the stairs*, she thought.

She spent a few more minutes looking around, trying to imagine the tree falling. Then she ran back down the steps to Bess. "Where's Wayne?" she asked.

"I think he just took a load of stuff out to the truck," Bess said. "He'll probably be right back."

Nancy and Bess looked through the rubble for the

cleats, but didn't find any. When Wayne returned, Nancy ran to him. "I need to ask you some questions," she said. "Could we talk privately?"

"Well, just for a few minutes," he said. "There's so much to do, and the mansion this evening . . . It's a disaster, just a disaster!"

Nancy led him around to the side of the mezzanine steps. It was the same place she'd landed when she leaped to safety.

"What is it?" Wayne asked. "I'm glad you'll be onboard this evening, by the way. You're very creative. I'd love to have you consider joining us full-time next summer."

"Thanks," Nancy said, smiling. "I want to talk to you about the accident."

Wayne's face resumed the distressed look he'd had for the last several hours.

"What really happened, do you think?" Nancy asked. "I remember when we secured the tree with your special cleats. What failed?"

"I've been thinking about that ever since it happened, Nancy," Wayne said, his voice taking on a hushed tone. He looked around to make sure no one could hear. "I'm going to have to have some answers for the insurance companies—you can bet on that."

"Was it the cleats, the ones you designed?"

"No!" he proclaimed, his voice a little firmer. "Absolutely not! I designed those to be totally fail-safe. I refuse to believe they were the problem. It must have been the fastenings in the floor—the eye-bolts maybe, or the floorboards."

"So you think someone just bumped into the tree near its base, and it mysteriously pulled loose?" Nancy wondered.

"Maybe a waiter with a full tray for the tearoom," Wayne offered. "He couldn't see where he was going, and he just fell into it."

"Has anyone found any of the cleats yet?"

"I don't know," Wayne said. "Nancy, I've got to get back. There's *so* much to do. Bess didn't get lunch yet, so I'm letting you two leave now for a combined lunch and supper break. See you later." Wayne hurried off. "Dress casually," he called back. "We'll be working hard to get finished."

Nancy and Bess left the store and went home to change into sweaters and jeans for the evening shift. Finally they met at their favorite Mexican take-out place, picked up fajitas and burritos, and went to George's.

"I didn't think you'd ever get here," George said. "I want to hear everything!"

Nancy and Bess got George up to date. First they described the chaos of the accident scene. Then Nancy told them about the latest theft from the electronics department and her discovery in the stockroom.

"Whoa!" George said. "Jack's right. This is a much bigger operation than we thought."

"And done by someone very clever," Nancy pointed out. She took a bite of a fajita and then told them about her talk with Wayne.

"There's something really fishy about how the accident happened," Nancy told the others. "If there was enough force to pull the tree away from those eyebolts, they should show some kind of stress. There'd be some sign that they'd been pulled on. The eyebolts would jiggle, or the floor would be cracked or splintered."

"Wayne said the fastenings must have given way," Bess said.

"Not the ones in the floor," Nancy said.

"And as far as the railing goes, the cleats were fastened directly to it," Bess recalled.

"Well, we know the railing didn't give out, right?" George said, taking a sip of her soda.

"It must have been the cleats," Bess said sadly. "They must have failed, and he's too ashamed to admit it. Poor Wayne—this could ruin him."

"Maybe," Nancy said, gazing out the window.

"What are you thinking?" George asked.

"Bess, you were up on the mezzanine when it happened," Nancy said. "Did you see anyone near the tree? Did anyone bump into it?"

"No," Bess answered. "It was so huge, I couldn't

see if anyone was behind it—but I didn't see anyone fall over into it or anything. Why?"

"What if the fastenings *didn't* fail?" Nancy wondered. "What if it wasn't an accident?"

"Nancy," Bess said, putting down her burrito. "Are you saying what I think you're saying?"

"As securely as that tree was anchored," Nancy said, "there's no way it was going to fall just because someone bumped into it. And even if someone did, that shouldn't have made *all* the fastenings fail at the same time."

"Are you saying that someone . . ." George trailed off, deep in thought.

"Cut the wires and pushed the tree," Nancy finished.

Bess gasped. "And aimed it right at you!" she whispered.

Nancy jumped up. "I'm going back to the store," she said. "I have an idea."

"I'll go with you," Bess said.

"No, stay and finish your dinner," Nancy urged. "If I get stuck, I want at least one of us to make it to the Albemarle mansion. If I don't get back in time, you can drive George's car over, and I'll meet you there. Okay with you, George?"

"Sure," George said. "I just wish I could go too"

Nancy drove back to Albemarle's. She locked her backpack in the car trunk and went into the store.

She went straight up to the supply closet on the mez-zanine—the closet where the holly tree decorations had been stored. The door was locked. Nancy knew there were too many people around to risk using her lock pick, so she raced to find Diedra.

"Diedra, I need your help," Nancy said. "Do you have keys for the supply closets in the store?"

"Sure," Diedra said. "All the managers do."

"I need to get into one on the mezzanine, the one Special Effects used. And I don't want any of the decorators to know about it. Will you help me?"

"I can do that," Diedra said. "And I won't ask any questions. Ali told me about all you've done in the past few days. It's pretty awesome."

"Thanks," Nancy said as they walked to the mez-zanine.

Diedra inserted a key into the doorknob and opened the closet. She shielded Nancy while she stepped inside.

"You don't have to stay," Nancy said. "You could leave the keys with me. I'll lock up when I leave and return them to you."

"Okay," Diedra said. "This has one of those old-fashioned locks. It's probably been here since the store was built. You can't unlock the door from the inside, and you can only lock the outside with a key."

Nancy thanked her again, and Diedra left.

Inside the closet, Special Effects boxes were scattered everywhere. Nancy dug through the piles and opened nearly every box, but all she found was tissue paper, bubble wrap, and a couple of extension cords.

Finally she reached the back corner of the top shelf. Her fingers closed around a wooden box, and it rattled when she pulled it down. Inside the box was a set of cleats exactly like the ones used to secure the holly tree.

Nancy started piecing together bits of information. It was like assembling a jigsaw puzzle: one fact didn't fit, but another one did. Suddenly all the pieces of the puzzle seemed to scatter in her mind. A sharp pain seared through her brain.

She reached up to the back of her head and felt a lump starting to swell. Before she could turn around, the closet door slammed shut. It was totally dark.

12

Mistletoe and Folly

As the sharp hot pain in Nancy's head started to subside, she took a deep breath. *Well, I'm not unconscious,* she told herself. *Whoever tried to knock me out didn't quite finish the job.*

She tried the doorknob and wasn't surprised to find that the door was locked. Nancy remembered what Diedra had said about not being able to unlock the door from the inside. Diedra's keys were lying on the floor, but they were useless. There was no keyhole in the door at all.

Nancy knew she could pound on the door and someone would eventually hear her, find some keys, and let her out. But she wanted to avoid making a scene if she could.

Relieved to find her own keys in her jeans pocket,

she switched on the small light attached to the key ring. The first thing she noticed was that the cleats and the wooden box that held them were gone.

She immediately turned her attention to the task of getting herself out of the closet. She needed to find something in the closet to help her get out—maybe something that she could use to remove the knob from the door?

Just then she remembered the unused extension cords she'd seen earlier. She searched all through the boxes and paper and finally found them. With a good amount of force, she bent a prong of one of the plugs. Using it as a screwdriver, she undid the metal plate that held the knob in the door. After a few jiggles the lock disengaged, and the doorknob fell into her hand. The closet door swung open.

There was no one nearby, so she took the time to refasten the doorknob with just two of the screws. She was now able to close the door and lock it. Nancy then raced to WAVE, returned the keys to Diedra, and hurried out to her car.

It took twenty minutes for Nancy to drive out to the Albemarle estate. The rest of the Special Effects crew was already there.

"Oh, good, you're here," Cass said as she ran to meet her. "Hang your coat in here," she said, pointing to a large open coat closet in a small alcove off the foyer. "This place is like a morgue. No one's here except the servants. And Wayne is so depressed because of the accident this afternoon."

"I can see why he would be," Nancy said, following Cass into a very long room full of antique furniture. "He has a great reputation in River Heights. The accident could cripple his career."

Bess was waiting and happy to see Nancy walk into the long, two-story-high music room. Three separate sitting areas were arranged on three blue-and-ivory Chinese rugs. Along one wall, large windows were draped in blue velvet. Oil paintings of flowers and birds hung on walls draped with ivory silk. At one end of the room there was a large stone fireplace topped by a mirror in a wide gold frame.

"Isn't this *gorgeous*?" Bess asked. "I'm glad you're finally here, Nancy."

"It's a little too much for me," Cass said, shaking her head. "You can tell this place cost a bundle."

At the end of the room opposite the fireplace stood a grand piano and a harp. Both were ornately painted with flowers and gold vines. Next to them stood a two-story Christmas tree covered with lights and hundreds of flowers, which matched the ones on the piano and harp.

"Hello, you two," Wayne said as he hurried into the room. "I'm so glad you're here. Nancy, are you okay after the tree disaster? I'm certainly not. Frankly, I'm devastated."

"I'm okay," Nancy said. "What do you want us to do here?"

"We are going to absolutely wow the Albemarles with their estate decorations," Wayne said. "Maybe this will help redeem Special Effects a little." His voice sounded a little shaky.

"As you can see, we already have this tree outfitted with lights," he pointed out. "And we've added flowers to match the musical instruments. I've created these vines to match the vines on the instruments." He walked over to one of several circular cartons stacked on the floor and took out several coils of gold vines with gold silk leaves.

"I want you and Bess to twine these around the tree, like so." He took the end of one vine and pushed it deep in, toward the tree trunk. Then he brought it out to the edge, weaving it in and out of the branches. "Try to make the tree decorations match the paintings on the instruments."

He pointed to a door in the corner of the room. Nancy could barely see it, because it had been covered with the same ivory silk as the walls. "There's a stepladder in the closet over there. Are you both okay with getting up on a ladder after your scaffolding scare?"

"I am," Nancy said. Bess looked a little apprehensive. "I'll do the ladder—Bess can stay on the floor."

"Okay. After you're finished with that, I need you to do the windows. The other two cartons contain the garlands of mistletoe and ivory ribbon that you two braided," Wayne said. "I want them draped over the paintings and mirrors. Let me know when you're finished, and I'll come check your work. Then we'll move you upstairs. Cass, come with me."

As soon as Wayne and Cass left the room, Nancy told Bess what had happened in the mezzanine closet.

"Oh, Nancy, that's awful," Bess said. "Should you have a doctor check the bump?" she asked, parting Nancy's hair in the back.

"I'm feeling pretty good right now," Nancy said. "Even the headache has gone. I'll let you know if I think I'm in trouble."

"Who do you think it was?" Bess asked. "Why would someone want to steal those cleats Wayne designed? I don't get it."

"It's like a puzzle with just one missing piece," Nancy said. "But it's the most important piece—and there's no picture without it. Let me think about it while we're working. We can talk it over later." She could hear voices in the nearby rooms. "I really don't want anyone to overhear us now," she added.

Nancy got the ladder from the closet. It took them

less than an hour to finish decorating the tree. It was gorgeous. The tree looked especially beautiful next to the musical instruments.

Next they turned to the mistletoe decorations. Occasionally they heard enthusiastic voices and laughter from other parts of the mansion. "Sounds like everyone is starting to feel a little more cheery," Nancy commented.

"Yeah," Bess said. "Maybe it'll all turn out okay after all. I'd hate to see Special Effects fold just because of a couple of random accidents."

Nancy and Bess finally draped the last mistletoe garland over one of the oil paintings. "We still have one small painting and the big mirror over the fireplace to do, but we're out of mistletoe," Nancy said. "I'll go see what Wayne wants us to do."

When Nancy reached the foyer, she heard most of the voices coming from the floors above. She started up the stairs, then noticed one of the decorators in the dining room who was arranging the table centerpiece. Nancy had seen him a few times around the store.

"Hi," Nancy said. "We're out of mistletoe in the music room. Are any of the other decorators using it? We need only a few coils."

"I don't think so," he said. "But I was just out in the truck, and I know there's some in there. Just get what you need."

Nancy thanked him and went out to the parking area behind the house. The Special Effects truck was the size of a medium moving van. Inside, Nancy found a jumble of boxes, trays, and bags. There were two cartons with the word "mistletoe" scrawled on the side in black ink.

The first carton was sealed and very heavy, so she opened the other one. There was just a small clump of a coil lying on the bottom of the carton. *That might work for the small painting*, Nancy thought. She reached in and pulled it out. The ivory ribbon woven into the mistletoe was badly stained. Something about the color of the stain was familiar.

The only illumination in the truck shone in from the huge security lights bordering the parking court. Nancy took the mistletoe out of the truck and took it over to a spot directly beneath one of the security lights. The stain on the ribbon was a bright magenta.

13

Up on the Housetop

Nancy's mind filled with images and questions. She remembered what the saleswoman, Mary, had told her about the bright magenta stain that squirted from the security tags when they were tampered with. She also remembered how Jack had confirmed this when Nancy showed him the stains in the electronics department stockroom.

It was the same color as the stain on this ribbon, she thought. *Could this possibly be from the same source?*

Nancy pocketed the clump of mistletoe with the stained ribbon, locked the van, and hurried back into the mansion. She darted into the closet off the foyer and placed the mistletoe in her backpack. She then went directly to the music room where Bess was waiting.

Nancy's mind churned with ideas and scenarios. The puzzle pieces were beginning to fit together. She decided not to mention to Bess what she'd found until she had thought some more about it. She wanted to work out some of the questions in her mind before she brought them up to anyone else.

"Well, no luck," Nancy said to Bess. "I couldn't find any more mistletoe. We'd better ask Wayne what he wants to do with the small painting and the mirror over the fireplace."

"I think everyone's upstairs," Bess said. "It's gotten really quiet down here."

"Let's go find them," Nancy said.

They walked up the large curving staircase, which Special Effects crew members had wound with green garlands and blue-and-white bows. Nancy followed the sound of voices to the upper sitting room.

"Ahh, the music room is done!" Wayne announced with a sigh when he saw them.

"Not exactly," Bess said, explaining that they had run out of mistletoe.

"There must be something we can do," Wayne said, rushing out of the room. "I'll find enough for the small painting, and then I'll design a magnificent swag for the mirror. It will be stunning," he called back as he clambered down the stairs.

Nancy and Bess pitched in to help the crew finish decorating the Albemarle's sitting room. Nancy was still thinking about her discovery in the Special Effects truck. *Could Wayne possibly be involved with the thefts of electronic equipment from Albemarle's?* she wondered. Her thoughts were interrupted by Wayne when he returned to the sitting room.

"All is well," he announced. "I finished the decorating in the music room. After we're done here, let's take care of the ballroom." He went into the room next door—the upper kitchen.

Nancy heard Wayne rattling cups and running water, and she followed him into the galley-shaped room. Wayne was staring out the window, drinking a cup of coffee.

"So did you find more mistletoe?" she asked.

"No, I just made a swag out of boughs for the mirror," he answered, his back still toward her. "Then I cut some lengths off of the pieces on the other paintings, pieced them together, and draped that over the small oil painting."

"That's cool," Nancy said. She poured herself a glass of cider from the gallon jug the house staff had put out for the crew. "I love what you've done with the decorations. They're just beautiful. This is a great house."

Wayne turned and faced her. "Yes, it is. Glad you could give us a hand."

Nancy smiled warmly. "Me too. I'd never been here before. I wasn't sure I could make it after the accident," she added. She steered the conversation to the holly tree so she could ask him a few questions. "You know, seeing that tree come at me was pretty weird."

"I'm sure it was." He looked intently at her, but didn't smile.

"Were you on the floor when it happened? Did you see it fall?" she asked. "It was quite a sight."

"No," he answered. "I wasn't even in the store. I was finishing the swags for the store's front doors. I was horrified when I heard what happened."

"How did you find out?"

"Cass told me," he said. "She came to get me."

But I saw Cass, Nancy reminded herself. *She was up on the mezzanine with Bess, Diedra, and Ali. No way could she have gotten out to you.*

"It's so odd that the cleats haven't shown up since the accident," Nancy said. "They would be good evidence for the insurance company of how careful you were to secure the tree. But you probably have some extra ones around."

"Actually, I don't," Wayne said. "They were custom made, and pretty expensive. They were the only ones I had."

A picture of the wooden box of cleats in the mezzanine closet came instantly to Nancy's mind.

Wayne put down his cup abruptly. "You know what? We need to get back to work. There's still a lot to be done around here." He walked quickly past Nancy and left the kitchen.

Nancy rinsed out her glass and followed Wayne into the sitting room—but he wasn't there. She walked over to Bess, who was placing porcelain figures on a miniature ice rink. "Where's Wayne?" Nancy asked in a low voice.

"I don't know," Bess answered. "He kind of raced out of the room. Isn't this park scene cute?"

"Come on, let's go," Nancy said. She and Bess hurried out of the room. They started in the hallway gallery, then they wound in and out of corridors, bedrooms, sitting alcoves, playrooms, a media room, and an office. But there was no sign of Wayne.

Finally Bess stopped. "Nancy, where are we going? What are we doing?"

Quickly Nancy told Bess about finding the magenta-stained ribbon in the truck. "Just now, when I asked him who told him about the holly tree accident," she added, "he told me that Cass had gone outside the store to get him."

Bess thought for a moment, then spoke. "But that can't be. Cass was up on the mezzanine with us. We couldn't get down until the tree was pulled out of the way. So we stayed up there and tried to calm everybody down. By the time Cass and I got down the steps, Wayne was already there."

"Exactly," Nancy said.

119

"So he must be mistaken about who went out to tell him."

"Maybe."

"Nancy, what are you saying?" Bess asked. "That Wayne lied?"

Nancy told Bess about finding the cleats in the closet and how she'd caught him in another lie. "Either he lied when he said the holly tree cleats were the only ones made, or he lied when he said they weren't found after the accident," Nancy pointed out.

"Whoa," Bess said, shaking her head. "I don't get this."

"I don't either," Nancy said. "But I'm trying to figure it out." She turned her head. "Quiet. . . . Listen," she instructed Bess in a whisper. Bess cocked her head in the direction Nancy pointed.

There was no mistaking Wayne's voice, even when he spoke in low tones. Nancy cautiously followed the sound up a narrow staircase to the third floor. Bess followed.

They hugged the wall opposite the banister, hiding in the shadows as much as possible. When they reached the second step from the top, Nancy stopped so she could check out where they were headed.

The staircase ended in the middle of a narrow corridor. There was a closed door directly ahead. Wayne's voice was coming from the right. Nancy gestured to Bess not to speak as they crept up the last couple of steps to the corridor.

"I know—I know what I told you," Nancy heard Wayne say. His voice came from a large, brightly lit room at the end of the hall. The high, arched entrance to the room was draped in green velvet pulled back by cream-colored fringe and tassels. Through the arch she could see a large white-and-gold chandelier shaped like a seashell. The floor was beautifully finished hardwood, with an inlaid pattern of shells.

Nancy quickly assessed the situation. She pointed toward the room where Wayne was talking and silently mouthed the word "ballroom" to Bess, who nodded. There were several doors between Nancy and the ballroom. Most of them were closed. The room next to the ballroom was open, and it was completely dark.

Nancy made a split-second decision and led Bess down the hallway to the dark, open room. They ducked inside. It was easy to see where they were, because light spilled from the ballroom in a long beam across the floor. An arched opening separated the dark from the ballroom next door.

Nancy hugged a corner of the arched doorway, shielding herself with the velvet drape that hung from it. Bess took the same position on the other side of the doorway.

"Just be patient," Wayne said from next door.

Then it was very quiet. Even though he was at the far end of the room, the acoustics in the ballroom were so good that Nancy could hear him clearly when he spoke again.

"It will all work out," Wayne said. Then he was silent again. Nancy was sure that the periodic pauses meant he was talking on the phone, not to someone else in the ballroom. The soft velvet drape tickled her cheek as she leaned in closer toward the doorway.

"You'll get your money," Wayne said, and this time he sounded agitated. His voice was higher. "I know what our deal was—it was my idea, remember? But things are heating up a little, and I have to back off for a day or two. It'll all come together. Now get off my back. Wait—just a minute."

It was quiet again, and then Nancy heard a different sound—one that seemed to stop her heart in the middle of a beat. She could hear footsteps coming toward her. Nancy's legs felt as if they were melting into the floor and she'd never be able to move fast enough to escape.

When Nancy saw the fear in Bess's eyes, she jolted into action. Nancy looked around the small room. There was no closet, one window, and only two doors: the one they had used to come in, and the one where they were hiding. *If we run into the hall, he'll hear us or see us—or both,* she reasoned.

Motioning for Bess to follow, Nancy crept around the room to the window. She looked outside and saw a small balcony. Nancy pulled the old-fashioned brass lever down to unlock the window, and then pulled on the handle. Her pulse pounded so hard in her temples, she could barely hear the footsteps—but she heard enough to know they were still coming toward her.

She boosted Bess up and out of the window onto the little balcony. Then she hoisted herself up and out, pulling the window shut behind her.

As soon as she got her footing, she discovered they were not on a real balcony. Instead, it was one of those fake ones, attached only for decoration. Nancy's feet clung to a cement ledge only about a foot wide. In front of the ledge was a white iron railing.

The two girls balanced themselves on opposite sides of the window, pressing their backs into the cold stone of the house. Nancy turned her head toward the window, which gave her a narrow view back into the room. She saw Wayne come through the archway, walking in the beam of light from the ballroom. He still held the cell phone to his ear. He looked around the room, then turned to leave.

Nancy realized she had been holding her breath, and she was about to gulp some air, but movement at the corner of her line of sight made her continue to hold her breath. Wayne came back into the room and walked straight toward the window, frowning.

Nancy had held her breath for so long that she felt as if her lungs were deflating like a popped balloon. As Wayne neared the window, she shot Bess a warning glance before taking a tiny sip of air. . . .

14

The Trap Springs to Life

As Wayne walked steadily toward the window, Nancy and Bess pinned themselves even closer to the cold stone wall. From her viewpoint, Nancy watched Wayne. She didn't dare blink.

Wayne looked at the brass handle at the bottom of the window, still frowning. He grasped the lever and pulled it down to lock the window. Then he pulled the drapery shut.

It was very cold and very dark on the tiny fake balcony three stories from the ground. "Bess, are you all right?" Nancy whispered.

"Sure," Bess said. Nancy could tell that her friend was trying to sound cool.

Nancy scanned down the side of the Albemarle mansion. She saw more decorative balcony-type structures dotting the side of the wall. Every time she moved, cold stone scraped her back and cold iron grazed the front of her legs.

"Looks like that rock climbing I did last summer is going to come in handy," Nancy finally said. "Can you hold on here by yourself for a little while? When I get down, I can get the extension ladder from the truck for you."

"Sounds like a plan," Bess said. "Just hurry?"

Nancy climbed over the white railing and lowered herself down until she was hanging by both hands from two iron rails. Looking down and feeling around with her right foot, she found a jutting stone that she could use as a toehold. Then she angled her left side down until her left foot touched the top of a railing outside a second-floor window.

She tested the railing by pushing down with her foot. When she was sure that it would hold her weight, she released her left hand and found a rock farther down to grasp. She moved down the wall very slowly, using the stone wall and the fake balconies like rock-climbing ledges.

When she finally reached the ground, she raced to the Special Effects truck and brought out the extension ladder. It wasn't that heavy, but she had to move slowly. Carrying the ladder was awkward, and she didn't want to attract the attention of any-

126

one inside the house—especially Wayne Weber.

Nancy maneuvered the ladder to the side of the house. Bess climbed on and scrambled to the ground. The two girls rushed the ladder back to the truck, and entered the mansion.

They found no one on the first two floors. They climbed up to the third floor and found the decorating crew finishing up in the ballroom.

"I wondered where you were," Cass said. "We missed you."

"We were calling our friend George," Nancy said. "She had an accident the other day, and we wanted to check in with her." She looked around the room. "Where's Wayne?"

"I don't know," Cass said. "He disappeared about an hour ago."

Nancy and Bess picked up some greenery and garlands and blended back into the group. Soon Cass declared the ballroom done. Everyone picked up empty cartons and bags and trooped back down to the first floor.

Wayne greeted them all at the foot of the stairs. "Okay, everyone, time to pack up. Make sure all the gear and containers are back in the truck. I'll check the ballroom and be right back." He sprinted up the staircase.

Nancy, Bess, Cass, and the others began hauling

the last Special Effects things out to the truck. When everything was packed up, they left the Albemarle mansion. Nancy picked up George, and they drove to Brad's Beans, a great coffeehouse on the edge of town. A light snow started to fall.

"I need a double-mocha latte with cinnamon," George said, rubbing her hands together.

"And some chocolate-chip biscotti. Mmm!" added Bess.

While Bess and George ordered, Nancy called Ali and Diedra and asked them to come over. They arrived just minutes later.

Quickly Nancy told them all about her experience in the closet, her conversations with Wayne, the stained ribbon in the Special Effects truck, and the phone call she and Bess overheard.

"I can't believe it," Ali said.

"I know, I couldn't either when Nancy first told me," Bess said. "But then we heard him on the phone. He's obviously having money troubles. . . ."

"So that gives him a motive," George agreed.

"As Nancy says, he certainly had the opportunity to steal those things," Diedra added. "He pretty much has the run of the store while he's decorating."

"And the electronics thefts started about the time Special Effects moved in," Nancy said. She took a sip of her latte.

"What about the other stuff that's been happening?" Ali asked. "Do you think he's been behind that, too?"

"Diana confessed to taking the dresses from WAVE," Nancy said.

"And also to trying to break into your car and knocking into you in the stockroom," Diedra added.

"But there's been a lot more going on," George said, rubbing her sore knee. "Do you think Wayne pushed me down the escalator?"

"Diana was in jail at the time, so she sure didn't do it," Nancy pointed out. "And she insisted she didn't break into Bess's locker or leave that warning. Jack Lee thinks she's behind all of it—even the electronics thefts. But I'm not so sure."

"Are you going to tell Jack about your suspicions?" Ali asked, dipping an almond biscotti into her cocoa.

"Not yet," Nancy answered.

"We need more proof, right?" Bess said. A puff of whipped cream clung to her upper lip.

"Absolutely," Nancy agreed. "Look, Wayne's already in a lot of trouble with the holly tree accident—if it *was* an accident. He's going to have legal problems, insurance problems . . . If I'm wrong, and he didn't have anything to do with the thefts, it wouldn't be fair to dump that on him too. Sometimes when people are falsely accused, they never recover from it—even if they're proven innocent. I want more proof before I talk to Jack."

"What about the stained ribbon?" Diedra said. "That sounds just like the magenta stain from a security tag."

"Wayne's an artist," Nancy reminded them. "He's probably got a lot of magenta paint or dye around. Only a chemical analysis can determine whether the two stains are exactly the same."

"So you think the tree falling might not have been an accident?" George said.

"He lied about how he found out about it," Nancy said. "And his possible reasons for why it happened were pretty lame. That's why I went back to the store. That tree was huge. Someone could easily hide behind it before giving it a shove. Then, when everyone's attention followed the tree, the culprit could hide out in that supply closet."

"If the person *knew* about the closet," Ali pointed out.

"And had a key," Diedra added.

"Which, of course, Wayne did," Nancy said. "In fact, the closet is temporarily *his*. He's also the only person who could disconnect the cleats from the tree fast enough to make it look like an accident. I wanted to walk through the possible scenario and see what might turn up. Those cleats that I found in the closet would have been perfect evidence."

"I thought the holly tree was his masterpiece," Ali said. "How could he destroy it?"

"If there's anything I've learned from working on cases with Nancy," Bess said, "it's that people get desperate when they start feeling trapped." She turned to Nancy. "You said that Jack thought Diana might have an accomplice," Bess said. "Do you think she and Wayne might be working together?"

"I don't know," Nancy said. "We don't have anything connecting them—at least, not yet."

"If he was the one in the store that night—the one who pushed me," George said, coming to a conclusion, "he might have followed us and figured out that Nancy's been doing some undercover investigating. The tree wasn't the first warning he might have sent."

"Hey, that's right," Diedra said. "I almost forgot about the scaffolding."

Everyone sipped their drinks and seemed lost in thought for a few minutes. Then Nancy spoke. "Okay, here's the plan. Diedra, can you get us into the store after hours?"

"I can," she answered. "Managers have special swipe cards for that."

"When you use it, it probably registers your ID so Jack can check afterward and find out what employees were there after hours—and when."

"Right," Diedra said. "Some managers never come in that late, but I like to. I can get caught up on inventory and paperwork without being interrupted."

"Does it ring any kind of an alarm or signal when you swipe your card?" Nancy asked. "Is the new guard alerted if someone comes in?"

"No," Diedra said. "It doesn't register anywhere else besides the unit we swipe into. Only Jack can check later if he wants to."

"Great," Nancy said, checking her watch. "Is everyone free for the next couple of hours?" Nancy shared the rest of her plan with her friends, and they all agreed to help.

"George, you're up first," Nancy said. "You're the only voice we're sure that Wayne has never heard." She handed her friend a cell phone and a piece of paper with a few lines written on it. "You can improvise if you want—just make sure these basic things are said. Bess gave me Wayne's office number and his cell-phone number. Try the cell phone first."

George looked over the paper and then dialed. She nodded to the others, and said, "Wayne Weber? This is your new partner." She paused before speaking again. "It doesn't matter who I am. I work in Albemarle's electronics department. I know everything—and so will the police unless you cut me in."

She paused again before saying, "Look, I know about the boxes in the storeroom—the ones that you emptied and then sealed back up. I also know that we just got a new shipment . . . notebook computers . . . top of the line . . . easy to move, easy to sell . . . at least $1,500 each on the black market."

George grinned at Nancy, then spoke to Wayne again. "The store doesn't open tomorrow until noon. We can move the stuff from the store tonight, and it can be out of the state before it's even missed. . . . I'll meet you in an hour in your room in the basement. . . . I know the guard's routine, so I can take you upstairs when he won't be around." George clicked off the phone. "He bought it," she said. "Looks like you were right, Nancy."

"Good," Nancy said with a smile. "Diedra, we'll take your car. Albemarle's parking lot will be pretty empty, and he might recognize mine."

"I was going to suggest that," Diedra said. "Plus, if the guard checks, he'll see my manager's parking sticker and assume everything's okay."

Nancy, Bess, George, and Ali piled into Diedra's car, and she drove to Albemarle's. At the employees' entrance, Diedra took her special plastic card and swiped it through the metal slot by the door. The door opened with a slight click.

"Now, remember," Nancy said, "if we're caught, we've all got a story. Diedra and Ali are marking merchandise for tomorrow's sale. Bess, George, and I are picking something up for Special Effects. And one final warning: We don't know if Wayne carries a weapon. If there's any indication he might be armed, we scrap the plan. Follow my lead."

Once inside, they hurried down to the basement storeroom, and Diedra unlocked the door. When they started to hear footsteps in the hallway, Nancy turned off the light. Bess, Ali, and Diedra hid under the wraps with the mechanical figures. George pulled back into the shadows in the corner, just to the right of the door. Nancy stepped back into the opposite corner.

The door opened slowly with a spooky creak. Nancy saw Wayne Weber's head silhouetted in the hallway light. He stepped inside.

"Don't turn on the light," George whispered.

"Who are you?" Wayne asked.

"The one who called you about an hour ago," George said in a low voice. "Your new partner."

Wayne closed the door behind him and turned toward the corner where George stood. His back was to Nancy and the others. A thin green line of light from the top of the door shined above his head. "Have you told anyone else about this?" he asked.

"Nope," George said. "Where do we unload the stuff? I gotta know everything to protect myself."

"We go straight to Chicago," Wayne said. "I've got a contact there."

"Who is it?" George asked.

"You'll meet him tonight," Wayne said. "I called him before I got here."

"You're not working with anyone else, are you?

After all, your gig here with the decorating is going to be over pretty soon. I want to make sure I'm the only inside contact." George was doing a great job of asking everything Nancy told her to.

"No, you're it," Wayne said. "Now let me turn on the light. Standing here in the dark like this is creepy. I want to see my new partner."

"That's okay, Wayne, we'll get it," Nancy said, stepping from the shadows and flicking on the light. At Nancy's cue, Bess, Diedra, and Ali popped out from underneath the wrap. Diedra beeped Jack. Bess and Ali lugged a heavy, round carton in front of the door.

"What's going on?!" Wayne yelled. He whirled around a few times. His face turned bright red and his dark eyes flashed with shock.

"It's over, Wayne," Nancy said. "We know all about your money problems and what you've done to solve them. It's just too bad that such a creative mind was wasted on criminal schemes."

"Maybe I'll decide when it's over," Wayne said, his expression turning to fury. He leaped to the corner and grabbed George, twisting her arm tightly behind her. If she hadn't been injured, she'd have broken the hold. But Nancy knew she couldn't get any leverage with her leg in a cast.

Wayne dragged George toward the door, bumping her legs against the boxes. Nancy felt a sympathetic pang shoot through her when she heard George's soft moan of pain.

"She'll hurt a lot more if anyone gets in my way," Wayne growled. "Now clear that carton out of the way, and open the door."

15

Happy Holidays

"I mean it," Wayne said, his words rushed and loud. "Stay out of my way, or your friend here is going to have more problems than a leg in a cast."

The others took their cue from Nancy, who nodded. Diedra and Ali rolled the carton away from the door. Bess stood very still.

Wayne zigzagged around boxes and cartons. His grip on George seemed very tight, but it looked to Nancy as if he was having trouble keeping George's arm twisted and dragging her around at the same time.

"Everyone, get down," Nancy said, dropping to a sitting position on the floor. "Give him plenty of room."

As the others sat down on boxes or the floor,

Nancy inched backward toward the wall. One arm behind her, she scanned the floor until she found what she was looking for. She picked up the console unit behind her and plugged it into the wall.

"Wayne, you're making a mistake," Nancy said, starting a general patter to mask her activity. Wayne was circling around past her, moving toward the door. George's dragging feet got tangled up momentarily in the heavy drapes that had covered the mechanical figures. Wayne kicked the drapes away and headed for the door.

As Nancy rambled on, she leaned over and placed her hand on the brass lever. She held her breath, waiting for the right moment. Finally she pushed the lever.

With a whirring noise, the old iron figures came to life. Wayne jumped when he heard the noise, and he almost dropped George—but he quickly caught himself. Nancy's mechanical posse, though, was too much for him. The mother's arm hit Wayne's shoulder as it came up toward her mouth. He spun away just as the pony pulled the sleigh forward, trapping Wayne and George between the pony's shaking head and the father's bowing figure.

Wayne tried to kick the sleigh out of the way, but it kept moving. When it finally started backward again, Wayne dropped George and sprinted toward the door.

The policeman figure reached for the pony's bridle and landed a solid blow to Wayne's midsection. Wayne crumpled to the floor in surrender.

Wayne looked up at Nancy. His fury was gone, and only shock remained. "I don't know how this all happened," he mumbled. "How did everything get so out of hand? And how did you figure it all out?"

"There were lots of clues," Nancy said. "It just took a while to piece them all together. We overheard you on the phone in the Albemarles' ballroom," Nancy told him. "It sounded like someone was giving you a hard time about money."

She could hear someone coming down the hall, so she kept talking to distract him. "It must be awful to have someone pressure you like that."

"That's it!" Wayne said, looking up. He blinked several times. "Pressure. I was under a *lot* of pressure. Pressure to do a wonderful job decorating the store and the mansion. Pressure to keep the price down and meet the deadline. Pressure to pay off my loan," he muttered.

"Loan?" Nancy prompted.

"My business is in trouble," he said. He sounded scared. "I always wanted to use the best products, you know, the best equipment, the best details. I got farther and farther behind in my payments, and

I finally found someone to loan me a lot of money. And now it's due."

"So you decided to steal from Albemarle's," Nancy said. From the corner of her eye, she saw Jack quietly enter the room.

"Well, it was so easy," Wayne said with a smile. "I could be here any time I wanted. I bring in large cartons and bags full of stuff to decorate with. Instead of taking these containers out empty, why not use them to smuggle out merchandise—expensive stuff I can sell to help get this guy off my back?"

Wayne noticed that Jack had joined them. "I suppose you heard all this," he said to Jack. "By the way, those security tags with the exploding dye are pretty smart. When that first one went off, it was a major shock. I had plenty of time to figure out how to disable them, though. I even had the supplies and equipment I needed to reseal the boxes so that no one could tell they were empty," Wayne added. "All in all, it really was a perfect plan."

Bess shook her head while she listened.

"Don't you shake your head at me," Wayne said to her, his voice taking on a sudden tone of anger. "It *was* a perfect plan until your friend here got in on the act." He scowled at Nancy. "When you started snooping around, it messed everything up. I wanted to fire you and Bess right away, but that would have just made things worse. What's the old saying—keep your friends close, and your enemies closer? I knew I needed to keep an eye on you."

"Did you leave that warning in my locker?" Bess asked.

Wayne nodded. "I saw Nancy asking questions in the electronics department. That's when I first suspected that she might be looking into the thefts there. I thought that ruining something of hers might scare her off the case. I didn't know which locker you'd given her, though, so I broke into yours. I knew she'd get the message."

"And when that didn't work," Nancy guessed, "you sent us up two stories on that scaffolding—"

"And then pulled a few screws out of one corner." Wayne finished her sentence. "I didn't mean to actually bring it down. But when it collapsed, I thought that would surely be the end of your little undercover investigation."

"You don't know Nancy very well," George said with a chuckle.

"No, I didn't—then," Wayne said. "I was amazed that hanging you up on that clock only seemed to increase your commitment to being a pain in my neck. I soon found out just how much trouble you could be when I was smuggling out a major haul and discovered you staking out the store."

Wayne was interrupted by a knock at the door. Jack opened it and ushered in a River Heights policeman. While the officer read Wayne his rights and handcuffed him, the decorator became quiet. But then he smiled again and turned to George.

"You're the one I tossed down the escalator, I'll bet," he said to her. "I didn't know at the time—didn't care. I was desperate at that point. I'd already stolen so much, it was too late to turn back. And I wasn't going to let a hotshot young detective get in my way. I had to get rid of you."

As he said "you," he looked into Nancy's eyes. She felt a clammy, cold rush. "I didn't know how or when, but I knew it had to happen," Wayne finished.

"And that's where the holly tree came into the picture?" Jack asked.

"It was pure luck," Wayne said. "I couldn't have planned it better. I was up there, finishing the last touches. My beautiful creation was finally done—ready for the world to see. I turned on the lights, then disconnected the screens. As I started to pull them away, I saw her walking up the steps."

"You were behind the tree," Nancy prompted.

"Right again," Wayne said. "Since I designed those security cleats, I knew how to spring them instantly. I waited for the perfect moment and gave the tree a shove. My spectacular tree . . ." He sighed. "But it was worth the loss, to get rid of you."

"Everyone's attention was on the tree, so no one

noticed you sneaking away," Nancy concluded.

"I hid out in the closet up there until I could escape," Wayne said.

"Just like Nancy thought," Ali said. Her soft auburn curls bounced as she nodded.

"What about Diana Herbe?" Jack asked. "Is she in on all this with you?"

"Who?" Wayne asked. "I don't know anyone by that name. I would never have trusted anyone to help me with any of this," he added. "Unless I was blackmailed into it—like tonight."

"And the cleats I found in the closet?" Nancy asked. "They're the originals from the holly tree?"

"Boy, you are like a dog with a bone when it comes to those cleats," he said. "Always asking me about the cleats. When I released them from the tree, I slipped them into my pocket. Things got so crazy—I just didn't want to be carrying them while we cleaned up. So I locked them in the closet. I planned to take them home tonight."

"But you saw me in the closet," Nancy said.

"I saw you two hanging around," He nodded toward Nancy and Diedra. "I couldn't let you take the cleats to the police. Any lab would be able to prove that they didn't have any signs of metal stress. It would have opened up a whole investigation into how the tree fell."

"Unfortunately for you," Jack said, "Nancy had already opened that investigation."

"Okay, it's time for us to go," the officer said, walking Wayne away.

Jack turned to Nancy. "We'll need statements from all of you. And I know the Albemarle family will want to express their thanks to you, Nancy. All of you go home and get some rest. I'll be in touch tomorrow."

"Oh—Wayne told us he sells the stuff to a man in Chicago," Nancy said. "He called him just before he got there. Be sure to check his cell phone for the last number he called. You can probably trace it."

By Sunday morning it had finally stopped snowing. Sunlight sparkled on the snow. Mrs. Albemarle called and invited Nancy, Bess, George, Diedra, and Ali to join her and Jack Lee at the Albemarle mansion for brunch.

Nancy pulled on her new red sweater and a white skirt, and she picked up the others at their homes. All of them were dressed in the same colors for the impromptu holiday brunch.

Jack and the Albemarles' butler met them at the door. "We traced that phone call made from Wayne's phone to Weber's fence in Chicago," Jack said. "There wasn't anyone there when the police arrived, but they're staking him out. It's just a matter of time.

Great job, Nancy! Now it's clear to me why you have such a good reputation as a detective."

Everyone assembled in the music room. Small tables for four and six were set with elegant linens, silver, and crystal. A buffet was set up on a sideboard between the windows. Fluffy scrambled eggs, roast turkey with raspberry sauce, and grilled vegetables stayed hot in ornate chafing dishes. Muffins and holiday breads were piled into pyramids, and bordered by sliced wheels of cheese. Compotes of fruit and trays of cookies were scattered around the room on side tables.

Jack introduced several Albemarle family members. They all expressed deep gratitude to Nancy and her friends. Finally, over tea and cakes, Mr. Albemarle addressed the whole group.

"Thank you, Jack," he began. "I've always said you're the best security chief in the business. You've proven me right." Mr. Albemarle turned toward Nancy and her friends. "We have all told you how much we appreciate what you've done," he said, looking at Nancy. "You have saved us money and heartache. The store has been in our family for more than one hundred years. It means much more to us than just a place of business. We haven't decided on the full extent of the reward we will offer you. There will be a monetary reward for each of you, but we would like to do more."

He turned to Diedra and Ali. "For you two, your loyalty to Albemarle's is exemplary. Diedra, we would like to offer you the position of store manager. We regret not having done so before. You deserved the job then, and you deserve it even more now. Please don't turn us down." Diedra smiled and took a deep breath.

"Ali," Mr. Albemarle said, "I know you're on the executive track, and we're very pleased that you have agreed to return to work after being mistakenly dismissed. I understand that you are also a designer. We haven't worked out all the details with the buyer yet—but to show our appreciation, we are going to place a few of your creations in a special display in WAVE." Ali seemed caught between glee and disbelief. Her eyes brimmed with tears.

"And now, Nancy," Mr. Albemarle said, "and your friends Bess and George. We're not sure what to do for you. You will each receive a gift certificate to Albemarle's, of course. We also want to specifically offer you each a gift from our electronics department to express our thanks."

After his speech, Nancy and her friends—both old and new—gathered to congratulate each other. "What tipped the scales, anyway?" Diedra asked Nancy. "What was the one clue that convinced you that it was Wayne?"

Nancy smiled and reached into her bag. She pulled out the mistletoe decoration with the bright magenta stain. Everyone laughed.

"Hmmm," Ali said. "Looks like he was roped by his own ribbon!"

EVERYBODY LOVES A MYSTERY!

How many of these chilling mysteries
from Aladdin Paperbacks have you read?

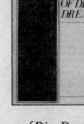

Evil Encounter by Sonia Levitin
0-689-80601-9

The House of Dies Drear by
Virginia Hamilton
0-02-043520-7

Mr. Was by Pete Hautman
0-689-81914-5

Wolf Rider by Avi
0-02-041513-3

Aladdin Paperbacks
Simon & Schuster Children's Publishing
www.SimonSaysKids.com

**Do your younger brothers and sisters
want to read books like yours?**

Let them know there are books just for *them*!

They can join Nancy Drew and her best
friends as they collect clues and solve mysteries in

T H E

N A N C Y   D R E W

N O T E B O O K S ®

Starting with
#1 The Slumber Party Secret
#2 The Lost Locket
#3 The Secret Santa
#4 Bad Day for Ballet

AND

Meet up with suspense and mystery

in The Hardy Boys® are: The Clues Brothers™

Starting with
#1 The Gross Ghost Mystery
#2 The Karate Clue
#3 First Day, Worst Day
#4 Jump Shot Detectives

Look for a brand-new story every
other month at your local bookseller

Published by Simon & Schuster

Step back in time with Warren and Betsy through the power of the Instant Commuter invention and relive, in exciting detail, the greatest natural disasters of all time. . . .

PEG KEHRET

THE VOLCANO DISASTER

Visit the great volcano eruption of Mount St. Helens, in Washington, on May 18, 1980. . . .

"Touching on some interesting problems in time travel, this fast-paced novel combines elements of fantasy with a disaster story. . . . A bibliography of books on volcanoes is appended."—*Booklist*

Florida Sunshine State Award Winner

THE BLIZZARD DISASTER

Try to survive the terrifying blizzard of November 11, 1940, in Minnesota. . . .

"Intriguing . . . high level of suspense. . . . Scenes described with chilling accuracy and the characters' emotional reactions are both realistic and moving."—*School Library Jounal*

"Science and historical fiction blend. . . . The resourceful kids [are] researchers [who] have material for a wonderful narrative report. . . . Fast paced and exciting."—*Booklist*

Iowa Children's Choice Master List 2000/2001

THE FLOOD DISASTER

Can they return to the past in time to save lives?

Iowa Children's Choice Award Master List 2000/2001

Available from Simon & Schuster